BEYOND LUCKY

SARAH ARONSON

Dial Books for Young Readers
an imprint of Penguin Group (USA) Inc.

DIAL BOOKS FOR YOUNG READERS
A division of Penguin Young Readers Group · Published by The Penguin Group

Penguin Group (USA) Inc., 375 Hudson Street, New York, NY 10014, U.S.A. · Penguin Group (Canada), 90 Eglinton Avenue East, Suite 700, Toronto, Ontario, Canada M4P 2Y3 (a division of Pearson Penguin Canada Inc.) · Penguin Books Ltd, 80 Strand, London WC2R 0RL, England · Penguin Ireland, 25 St. Stephen's Green, Dublin 2, Ireland (a division of Penguin Books Ltd) · Penguin Group (Australia), 250 Camberwell Road, Camberwell, Victoria 3124, Australia (a division of Pearson Australia Group Pty Ltd) · Penguin Books India Pvt Ltd, 11 Community Centre, Panchsheel Park, New Delhi - 110 017, India · Penguin Group (NZ), 67 Apollo Drive, Rosedale, Auckland 0632, New Zealand (a division of Pearson New Zealand Ltd) · Penguin Books (South Africa) (Pty) Ltd, 24 Sturdee Avenue, Rosebank, Johannesburg 2196, South Africa · Penguin Books Ltd, Registered Offices: 80 Strand, London WC2R 0RL, England

10 9 8 7 6 5 4 3 2 1

Library of Congress Cataloging-in-Publication Data

Aronson, Sarah.
    Beyond lucky / Sarah Aronson.
        p. cm.
    Summary: Twelve-year-old Ari Fish is sure that the rare trading card he found has changed his luck and that of his soccer team, but after the card is stolen he comes to know that we make our own luck, and that heroes can be fallible.
    ISBN 978-0-8037-3520-0 (hardcover)
    [1. Luck—Fiction. 2. Self-confidence—Fiction. 3. Soccer—Fiction. 4. Heroes—Fiction. 5. Teamwork (Sports)—Fiction. 6. Brothers—Fiction. 7. Jews—United States—Fiction.] I. Title.
    PZ7.A74295Bey 2011
    [Fic]—dc22
                                                                        2010028800

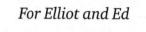

For Elliot and Ed

ONE

"I am a great believer in luck, and I find the harder I work the more I have of it."

—Thomas Jefferson

Jerry Mac MacDonald has no pre-game rituals. He wakes up, jumps out of bed, and eats whatever looks good. Even though we have to be on the soccer field in forty-five minutes, he shows up at my house and starts playing solitaire on my computer.

"You're not going to believe it, Ari. I just got the fourth king."

I believe it. Mac is the luckiest person I know. Beyond lucky. Always in the right place at exactly the right time. But it's not just that. Girls think he is cute. Two weeks of school, the guy still has no homework. Most impressive: Even though the stakes could not be higher, he does not feel out of control.

Today is the all-important last day of tryouts for Somerset Valley select soccer, U-thirteen, Division One. I can't leave anything to chance.

Call me obsessive, but first I eat a bowl of frosted

cornflakes with half a cup of puffed rice and one-third of a banana, because this is what I ate before the first time I kicked a ball over Mac's head. Under my jersey, I wear my brother Sam's U Mass T-shirt, the one I stole out of his trunk the day he announced to my family that he was dropping out of college to fight California wildfires. Since Sam is still the highest scorer in league history, I do the same fifty push-ups he did. Then I recite the American presidents in order, first to last, while I stare at the poster of my hero, Wayne Timcoe, the only Somerset Valley High player to ever make it to the pros.

Mac thinks this is over the top.

"But I love the presidents. Tons of great athletes and leaders have crazy superstitions."

"Not as many as you do." He has a point. But if they work, they don't have to make sense.

I sit on my bed and stretch my hamstrings. Before we leave, I would really like to read my daily horoscope as well as "Steve the Sports Guy: Real Advice for Real Men." But today of all days, the paper is late.

It's an extremely bad omen.

Mac shouts, "I win!" He turns off my computer, and we run downstairs. He is halfway to the front door when Dad notices that Mac's socks look like he's worn them all week, which he probably has, since his mom never does laundry until it is an emergency. "Put these on, Blondie," he says, reaching into a hamper and tossing Mac an extra pair. As we wait for him to change, Dad asks, "Are you ready to go?"

I stare at the empty curb, willing the paper to appear. If I am going to become Coach's starting keeper, I need to read it.

"Can we wait five more minutes?"

Five minutes becomes ten becomes fifteen, becomes "Come on, Ari, you don't need this. We're going to be late." We grab our gear, and my dad drives us to the field. All the way there, Dad showers us with his pearls of wisdom, the ones he never needed with Sam.

"If you play the way I know you can, Coach will have you both in the starting lineup. Just relax. You've worked hard. You are great players."

Mac started last year. He says to me, "You are going to be the next Wayne." Then he rolls down the window and waves to some random girls, who recognize him and scream his name. "There is nothing to worry about."

I must look extremely morose, because when we are near the gas station, Dad slows down. "Ari, would you like me to stop for a paper?"

"It's not the same."

"Then could we please lose the gloom and doom?"

Dad does not understand the truth about soccer. You can work hard. You can have great skills. You can want it more than anyone else on the field. But the stakes are high. Only one player can start at each position.

There is plenty to worry about.

Soccer is a battle, like solitaire or fighting a fire or even becoming the President of the United States of America. No matter how qualified or ready or experienced you are, you aren't going to get anywhere unless you are lucky. Timing is everything.

Confidence is essential.

When Coach tells me to cover the south net, the one facing the broken Exxon sign, the one Wayne Timcoe called his "Home, Sweet Home," Mac thinks everything's settled. "You see? Didn't I tell you? That's got to mean something."

More than anything, I hope he's right. I want today to be the day that Mac's and Sam's and Wayne's and every single decent president's luck rubs off on me and I play my best. Win. Maybe post a shutout. I want Coach to stop seeing Sam when he looks at me. I want him to call me the Teddy Roosevelt of soccer, because that's how tough I am going to play.

More than anything, I do not want to play backup ever, ever again.

All I need is a little luck.

I am the most unlucky person in the world.

We're ten minutes into our only split squad scrimmage of the day, the score is three to two, them over us, and the sun is in my eyes. Naturally, Mac has the ball. He zips down the center of the field straight at me.

POW!

"Goal!"

A well-kicked ball makes a sound like a pop. When it flies past your ear into the back corner of the net, it whines.

Mac raises both his hands and pumps his fists. Our friends celebrate. "Nice."

"Great job."

"Right in the sweet spot."

Mac and I shake hands. This is not because Mac feels guilty or because I think it is bad luck not to. Shaking hands with your adversary is Coach's number one most important mandatory rule, what he calls the Valley way. He says sportsmanship is a vital component of competition, but the last time Sam was home, he told me Coach only cares about stuff like this when he's got a questionable player on the team.

"Who are you calling questionable?" Sam and I were sitting around the kitchen table, making paper airplanes. Even though we were not supposed to launch anything in the house, I couldn't resist. The rapier is the perfect plane. It flies like a glider, but it is as precise as a dart.

Sam's airplane took a nosedive. "Do I really have to explain?" Not really. I knew he was talking about Mac. He said, "You know I love the guy, but you can't deny it. When he's not around to psych you out, your whole attitude changes."

That surprised me. "You can't blame Mac for being good."

Sam crumpled up the paper and started again. "I wouldn't, if he cared more about the team than his stats."

Now Mac punches me in the arm like one more goal is no big deal. I grab the ball out of the corner of the net. It is slippery and wet and covered in mud. Mac says, "I swear, Ari, that ball was a fluke."

"That would be your fourth fluke today."

I hurl the ball as hard as I can, but of course, it hits a soft spot and stops dead two feet in front of my fullbacks. Abel Mischelotti, last year's starting goalkeeper, sits on the bench right in front of my net. He yells, "Nice brick, Flounder. When are you going to learn how to throw?" His leg is in a red and white cast that starts at his ankle and ends at his hip. He points his crutch like a machine gun—straight at my head.

Mac says, "Don't listen to him. Stay focused," but he is the star of the team, good enough to play in the premiere league, if he wanted to. "Seriously, you're doing great. You know if your brother was here, he would say the same thing."

When someone says "Seriously," you know they're anything but. If Sam were here, he would not be losing to anyone, especially not Parker Llewellyn.

In the opposite net, she crouches low, keeps her feet moving the way all the best keepers do. She may be small, but she is also smart. She has already saved three goals outside the net.

Her throws are accurate.

In drills, she never drops the ball.

Parker moved here last spring, and after totally dominating the top girls' leagues, she petitioned the town and the league to play with us. She said, "I've played offense. I've covered the net. Now I am ready for a new challenge and some real competition."

Mac thought the whole thing was a joke—a publicity stunt. It didn't matter how amazing she was, no girl was ever going to play Division One. The league would have to turn her down flat—safety reasons—or locker room issues—take your pick! There were hundreds of good reasons to choose from.

But Parker is lucky too. The lady selectman was a big fan, and she figured it all out. She said on record, "Go ahead, Ms. Llewellyn, make us proud. Show those boys how the game of soccer is played."

Coach cannot give my job to a girl.

He blows the whistle, three long blasts. "Two more minutes. Let's see what you have left."

I keep my feet moving, ignore the taunts from the end of the bench, and count presidents. *Washington, Adams, Jefferson, Madison, Monroe.* The opposing team kicks the ball south and east past both lines of defenders, to the corner of my side of the field. It hits an orange cone and ricochets out of bounds. Coach runs into my blind spot. "Corner kick blue!"

A corner kick is always a threat, especially when the kicker gets it to the leading scorer right in front of the—

Pop!

The ball stings my hands right through the gloves. I point to Eddie Biggs. "This one's for you." Eddie may have a tendency to talk too much, but he's a great stopper—a smart defender and the best player on either defense. Some people make fun of him because he tapes his ankles all the way to the knees, but when I throw him the ball, he traps it—no problem—and kicks it clear across midfield, as far away from Mac as humanly possible. The guy is gold. He yells, "Let's go, yellow team. Find your lanes. Concentrate! You can do it!"

Two goals against one girl should not be so difficult.

But my offense is playing like they belong in Division Three. The ball flies wide, then short, then wide again. Parker comes out of the net—no problem whatsoever—and kicks the ball away, and it's a perfect kick, a booming kick, as good as any of mine. When it hits grass, Mac is in position. With a lane. And a line. And sixty-two seconds.

That's an eternity for a scorer like Mac.

Adams, Jackson, Van Buren, Harrison. If Mac wanted to, he could dribble the ball around midfield and call it a day. Or he could head the ball out of bounds. It's not like anyone would hold it against him. No one would blame him if he took off his blue vest, sat down, and let someone else challenge the net. But Mac's not wired that way. He is a natural born winner. He never turns down a spotlight or a scoring opportunity or a chance to be the hero. Even when it's against me.

He passes to Steve Campbell, aka Soup, who dribbles around one defender before passing the ball right back. Mac to Soup, Soup to Mac, crossing midfield, edging in. It really is beautiful. They already look like a team. Like winners. On the attack. I yell to the defense, "We've got twenty-seven seconds left." *Tyler, Polk, Taylor, Fillmore, Pierce*. "Fill up the lanes—keep your eyes on MacDonald—don't let him fool you."

But that's exactly what he does.

Just as two of my defenders take the bait and commit to blocking Soup, Mac passes the ball into the open space right behind Eddie. It's an effective strategy. Eddie's caught off balance. He can't retreat. Mac races ahead and continues to dribble the ball. Sam taught him this trick in my backyard.

It leaves nothing but air between him and me.

I keep my feet moving. My hands are up. He's going to go for it. But this is the home of Wayne Timcoe. This is his net. His field.

This is my chance.

I check his feet and then his eyes. If I can stop him, it will impress Coach and make me the starter. It will be the best kind of save. One on one. Him versus me.

Unless he is setting me up.

He could lure me over, just to get rid of the ball and let Soup try and score. Soup is an excellent athlete. Then again, he could look left and shoot left, kill the keeper with one swift kick.

What is it, Mac? What are you going to do? Are you going to kick it right or left? High or low? Into the corner or—

Jump!

The grass tastes like lettuce, but more bitter and stringy. Coach blows the whistle and Mischelotti yells "Yes" five or six times. Maybe more.

I put my head on the dirt. Game over.

My hands are empty.

TWO

In the wake of losing the most important scrimmage of my career to a girl, there are only a few things my friends can say:

"You have to realize they were playing her soft."

"There was no way you were going to win. Mac was on fire! The blue team had all our best scorers."

"You looked really strong. That last save would have been awesome."

Lying is a nice gesture friends make for friends, but winning means everything. I know what they're thinking.

"He stinks. He couldn't even beat Parker Llewellyn. Embarrassing."

"I heard his brother was a scoring monster. What happened to him?"

"We're sunk. Finished. We'll be laughingstocks. We aren't going to win a single game without Abel Mischelotti in the net."

• • •

If there was ever a person who deserved to break his leg in three places, that person was Abel Mischelotti.

Last year, the guy tormented me. He forced me to carry his gear. And get him water. Once he even made me clean his cleats. I used up a lot of karmic energy, dreaming of his immediate and untimely demise.

But in my fantasy—which I had no more than seventeen times—he broke his arm. One time he came down with mono. It wasn't a bad case—he didn't have to miss school. He definitely didn't have to go to the hospital. Even in my deepest dreams, the laser only disintegrated him one or two times.

But this is one of the strange things about real life: You never know when your number is up. Bad things happen to nice people and the lousy ones too. In real life, Mischelotti didn't get hit by a laser, but he got worse than he deserved. His last stand was more gruesome than anything I could imagine.

It happened one week ago.

It was the second day of the tryout, my first, because the day before, I'd had to go to services. It was Yom Kippur—the Day of Repentance—the biggest holiday season in the Jewish calendar, the World Cup for Jews. No one's allowed to miss that.

So I felt totally out of sync.

I was the only one on the field with a spotlessly clean shirt, the only person who didn't get to choose a number, the only player from last year's bench not to have the opportunity to test the field. Which was very unfortunate.

After eight straight days of rain, the grass was extremely slippery. There were bare patches everywhere. I said, "This is why man created turf."

Mac jogged in place, sending up a fine mist the color of mud. "Technically, I shouldn't have to be here."

"Technically?" That didn't make sense. We lived for soccer. I asked, "What's bothering you?"

He pointed to the Home of Wayne Timcoe sign. There was Coach, huddled up with Mischelotti. Mac said, "If he names him captain, I'm out of here." It was no secret—both Mac and Mischelotti wanted that honor bad.

I didn't remind him that Coach had yet to even say hello to me. "Stop acting like me. You're the obvious captain. He'd be crazy to give it to Mischelotti." Coach might be a little on the eccentric side, but he'd been Sam's coach too, and Sam said he was fair. I told Mac there was no reason to be pessimistic. "You know Coach never names a captain right away. He's just trying to—"

"Heads up!"

Umph!

A ball hit me square in the back. Mud flew everywhere. I looked across the field. "Biggs! I'm going to make you pay." I was just joking. Now my shirt was dirty. I looked like everyone else. When Coach called us to midfield, I ran as fast as I could.

"Listen up, men. I mean, men and Parker." Coach had a deep, scratchy voice. "Plant your feet. Watch out for the puddles. If you pull up a piece of carpet, please do me a favor and put it back where you got it."

Someone said, "Did he just say please?" There were thirty-six of us and only twenty-two spots. We weren't used to Coach being gender neutral. Or polite. A few of the guys laughed. It was sort of funny.

Not Parker. She raised her hand and volunteered to help him set up the cones for our first drill of the day. Mac rolled his eyes. "Look at her. She runs like a girl."

Mischelotti pushed Mac in the shoulder. "Stop talking and line up. If we're going to make a run at the state championship, we have to play together. You got that, MacDonald?" He acted like he was already the captain.

"Got it." Mac stepped on my foot. Hard. He was acting like me—letting everything and everyone get to him.

I crossed every one of my fingers behind my back, listed wartime presidents, and hoped that all of yesterday's repenting and praying and talking about missed opportunities would amount to something good. My horoscope that morning had told me to stop swimming with the current and take chances. It said: "Go forth, and explore." So when Coach caught my eye, I did something I had never done before: I raised my hand and asked him if he would like me to take a turn in the net too.

Unfortunately, Coach was Episcopalian. He was not in tune with the idea of giving me a new opportunity for the Jewish New Year. He was in no mood to take chances or explore. He said, "I might need you to play sweeper."

In other words, you are the backup. Dribble around the cones just like everyone else.

I hate dribbling around the cones.

The first time around, Mac scored. Parker dribbled surprisingly well, but lost control when she got close. I sprayed six players with mud and dirty water. "You're finished, Salmon Head," Mischelotti said.

On the second turn, Mac scored again. Parker kicked a nice shot just over Mischelotti's head. My ball flew straight into his hands. "You have to attack the corner," Mac said. "Place the ball just out of reach. Mischelotti won't dive this early in the morning."

On my next turn, I took Mac's advice. I dribbled left to right, and it would have worked out great, but when I tried to plant, I slipped in the mud. The ball skidded off to the side. I fell flat on my face two feet in front of the net.

Mischelotti clapped his hands. He came out of position and stood over me in the famous Wayne Timcoe pose: hands ready and knees bent. Then he flexed his biceps and growled, just the way Wayne did after every great save. He said, "Ari Fish, you'll be lucky to be anything but a sorry little backup."

Mac told me to stand up and get back in line. "If Coach would put Fish in the net, you're the one who would be the sorry little backup."

Before I could walk away, Mischelotti grabbed my shirt and pushed me hard. "Fish in the net?" he said. "That's funny."

Lucky for me, I did not fall. Luckier than that, I got out of the way. In retrospect, it was probably my best move of the day. When Mac and Mischelotti are mad, anything can happen.

That doesn't mean what happened next was premeditated. Mac would never take out another guy intentionally. He isn't like that. The truth is, it was a freak accident.

Or maybe it was fate.

As I got out of the way, Mac charged the net. He slipped in the mud and took off. Really, he flew. Top speed. For a second, he looked like a human airplane.

A missile.

On target.

Headfirst.

I will never forget that sound.

Like wood on fire or my uncle Leo's old air gun.

The impact of Mac's head on Mischelotti's leg sounded like shin guards snapping. An explosion.

Crack!

When I had the nerve to look up, Mac was heaving into the mud and Mischelotti was lying on his back. Everyone was crying.

Mischelotti's leg bone was sticking out of his leg.

The rest happened in slow motion.

Coach fainted. Mac wouldn't stop crying. I tried not to look at Mischelotti.

This was nothing like my dream.

In my dream, Coach stays upright. Mischelotti walks off the field. Coach tells the entire team, "Ari Fish will be our starter," and he says it like he's beyond happy, like I had always been part of his master plan.

In reality, Mischelotti was in surgery for three and a half hours. When Coach called, he said, "It looks like Abel will miss the entire season."

He did not say, "Get ready to start."

He did not say, "You are the man."

He did not say, "I have confidence in you."

Instead, he sounded like his season was going to be one of missed opportunity—over before it began. He sounded like, if he had the chance, he'd take anyone over me.

Even a girl.

THREE

"You can tell a lot about a fellow's character by his way of eating jelly beans."

—Ronald Reagan

When I get home, a plate of cookies sits on the kitchen table. They are my favorite cookies—black and whites— with thick icing, half chocolate and half vanilla—and white cakey bottoms. They are arranged in a circle with one in the middle. They look a whole lot like a soccer ball.

There is popcorn, too, and I bet a million dollars and a two-goal lead that there are glasses frosting in the freezer and a pot of homemade chicken soup in the fridge, the kind with lima beans, onions, and carrots, and little flecks of fresh parsley floating on the top.

Dad is the chef and owner of Central Station Fish and Steaks, home of the forty-two-ounce sirloin. He has always been a firm believer in the healing effects of food.

My favorite book, *Secret Lives of the U.S. Presidents,* sits on the table. It is open to Gerald Ford, the only president not to be elected. His most controversial decision was granting a presidential pardon to Richard Nixon for his role in the Watergate scandal.

"Hey, champ." Dad points to the plate of cookies and digs his thumbs into the muscles right below my neck. "Try one out. They're from the new bakery. Fresh."

Only a fool would let a fresh cookie go to waste. I take a bite. White side first.

He says, "We're thinking of ordering them for the cookie table at the oneg."

The oneg is the reception immediately following my bar mitzvah. My big day. The day I become a man. It is kind of like a big Jewish birthday party, except in my case, I will already be thirteen. My birthday is in February. My bar mitzvah's in May. This is because at Temple Emanu-El, the rabbi tells all the people with birthdays in winter to choose a date in spring. He says the travel is too iffy. For such an important occasion, God will understand.

I take another bite.

"What do you think?"

I think the white side should be slightly more lemony, but the texture of the cookie is perfect. "Isn't it a little early to start thinking about the lunch?" I have barely begun learning to chant Hebrew from the Torah.

Dad digs into the popcorn bowl for the partially popped kernels at the bottom, which he swears are a delicacy. "It is never too early to start thinking about lunch."

Crunch.

With a big let-me-be-your-hero, I-understand-what-you're-going-through smile, he turns his chair around and rests his hands on the top of the bars, like he's Sam and not Dad, and he wants to talk sports and not failure. "So. Could you put your old man out of his misery, and tell me what happened? How did it go?"

I shrug. "It was fine."

"Fine, fine?"

"Just fine."

"Not fine as in great?"

"No, Dad. Just fine. As in fine." As in, let's talk about something else. He has to know that *fine* is the word people use when they don't want to talk. "Did you know that Grover Cleveland was a draft dodger?"

"What is the world coming to when we can elect someone like that?" My mother walks in, kisses his cheek, my head, and throws her keys on the table. "What a day!" She slumps into her seat and shakes her hair out of the blue nurse practitioner's net. "Three accidents. One facial laceration. And a pretty ugly grade three concussion." She zeroes in on my muddy footprints, takes the rag, cleans up the mess, and goes to the stove to boil water. "Adrenaline junkies." Her yellow scrubs are stained. Dark under the pits. A splattering the color of rust on the front. She washes her face in the kitchen sink.

My dad hands her a cookie. He no longer asks her where the stains come from. "Try this."

She eats the chocolate side first, gives it an enthusiastic thumbs-up. "Do you realize that's sixteen accidents this month? All men. Eighteen to twenty-four. It makes me crazy." After a few more case reports, she either smells me or notices my dirty soccer jersey. "How was the scrimmage?"

Dad shoots her the don't-ask, I'll-tell-you-later look, but she doesn't get the message loud or clear. "Well? What happened?"

"It was a disaster."

She squeezes my shoulder. "I'm sorry. I know soccer means a lot to you. You worked hard for today. And I know you thought that you had a real solid chance." I stare at Gerald Ford's large forehead. "But if your best isn't good enough for Coach," she says, letting go and picking up another cookie, "well then, so be it."

So be it—the loser's mantra.

The teakettle whistles.

Dad jumps up to pour her a cup. He says, "I know you won't believe this, but Sam used to go through the same drama every season. Remember, Marjorie? Every year, he'd sit by the phone, sure he'd messed up and that he was going to be cut. He would tell us about some other player who was bigger or stronger, and he looked exactly the way you do now. But the point is: He never was cut. He was always—"

"Dad, don't you get it? I lost. Five to two. To Parker Llewellyn." They should understand how bad that is. "All my friends are going to start except me."

My dad sighs in defeat. Mom sips her tea. She tells me,

for about the hundredth time, that people excel at different rates and at different times of their lives and that it would be awful if the best time of my life was happening right now. When this does not perk me up, she says that just because Sam did something well doesn't mean I have to follow in his footsteps. And that if I don't make the team, it could be a blessing in disguise, which, in my opinion, is one of the worst, most overused expressions in the entire English language.

I say nothing.

So she tells me that there are things more important than soccer. Like school. And Hebrew. "You need to call Rabbi," she says. "Have you even started studying your Torah portion?"

I should just say yes. Yes, I have. I should say I am well on my way to making them the proudest parents in Temple Emanu-El history. But I cannot lie, so I stare at a green spot on the table while she talks about things like commitment, preparation, and not putting myself behind the eight ball.

She says, "You need to get your priorities straight." And loosen up. And then, in my spare time, stop and smell the roses. But most of all, I need to stop comparing myself to Sam. "You have your own fantastic, worthwhile strengths."

That's enough. I grab this morning's newspaper, the one I should have read earlier, a couple of cookies, and stomp up the stairs. Slam my bedroom door shut.

From my room, I hear her yell, "Ari, come back! What did I say?"

Neither one of them better follow me up here. Or say anything about a silver lining or learning from my mistakes. Sometimes there's no good side.

Sometimes it's easier to face the facts.

I lost.

Parker won.

Sam is great at everything.

I'm not.

Alone, I refold the newspaper, so I can open it the way I would have, if it had arrived on time.

The front page is all about bad news. The president has made a speech. The economy looks bad. One hundred and sixty-two fires are burning in California alone. The paper reports the worst one is near Yosemite, and already a lot of people have had to evacuate their homes. Since Sam is a smokejumper, I know he's not anywhere near that fire. Sam says that smokejumpers hardly ever fight the big ones that make the news. They mostly jump into small remote fires—the kind that two or three men can overcome. When I think about it, smokejumpers are sort of like keepers. Their job is to catch the fire, or contain it, before it gets big.

This is pretty ironic, because Sam and I are nothing alike. Even though he loved Wayne Timcoe as much as I did, he would never have played keeper. "Play offensive midfield, or at least, the wing," he said when he first saw my gear. Of course, Mac agreed. "I hate to break it to you, but the only time anyone notices the keeper is when he messes up."

Mac could have held off on that last goal.

I turn the page. More bad news. In the middle of page three, there is a hole in the paper, a large square cut out and loose ends.

Every time a young person dies—in war, fire, or other selfless act—my dad cuts out the obituary and saves it in the top drawer in the kitchen next to the silverware. Last time I checked, he had seventeen. I guess it's his version of knocking on wood—warding off bad luck. Most are from the wars—Iraq and Afghanistan. But one lost his life fighting a huge fire near L.A. He was from Framingham, and he got a bridge named after him, which would be sort of cool if he didn't have to be dead to get it.

After my dad reads about a death, he always goes to the kitchen, and if he thinks no one's looking, he cries. He cooks something comforting. Like stew. Or he roasts a chicken. Then he writes the family a letter. He says that parents want to know that someone has read about their child, and he must be right because most of the time, the people write back. They thank him for writing and honoring their son's or daughter's sacrifice. A few times, they sent pictures. Smiling faces on sunny days. Often with a girlfriend or a dog or a brother.

Once, the dead soldier reminded me of Sam. Same wide

forehead. Same crooked smile. Same cocky expression.

I don't like thinking about that soldier. I don't want to know if he had a brother or a girlfriend or a team. I don't want to know if my dad thinks that someday we will get a letter about Sam. If that is why he cries. If he thinks it is just a matter of time.

My parents never tempt fate directly. The what if's and the why's are strictly off-limits and out of bounds. When people ask, "How can you stand to let your son fight forest fires? I thought he wanted to go to med school," my dad clenches his fists. My mom walks away.

They never say "Shut up," or "Why do you need to know," which is what Steve the Sports Guy suggested to someone in the same boat. They never say "We wish he hadn't volunteered."

But when I read about walls of flames or fire tornadoes or smoke inhalation or helicopter crashes, my hands shake. I wish my brother could be a safer kind of hero.

I lie down on my bed and stare at the ceiling. I hope Sam is okay.

I will never forget the night Sam decided to fight wildfires. He was already in college and everything he did seemed gigantic. His muscles were big. His hair was big—like a girl's—long and shiny and tied back in a ponytail.

At first, it was just supposed to be a summer job.

Back then, Mac lived with us, to help out his mom,

who supposedly went away to school. I now know this was a white lie. That actually, she was in some kind of program that no one talks about.

I didn't mind. I liked having Mac sleep on the cot in my room. Every night, we snuck downstairs to raid the refrigerator. We spent each afternoon and weekend kicking the ball or fishing or hanging out at the playground. We made an entire fleet of paper airplanes. We talked a lot about Sam.

The night he made his big announcement, my parents sent Mac and me outside. We ran around the yard and saved each other from imaginary burning houses. Mac thought Sam was the coolest, most exceptional person in the universe, and he could not understand why my parents were so mad. "Firefighters are heroes," he said. "They're like Superman and Batman, except they're real."

I had to explain to him: Sam was not *like* Superman. He *was* Superman.

Later, after my mother had stopped crying, we all sat around the kitchen table, and stared at the map of California. Sam pointed to a spot in the middle of the state and drew a large red dot. "Please Mom, don't wig out. I can handle it. Besides, it's just for the summer."

The dot bled.

Sam had been a volunteer fireman, but he hadn't seen any real action. He said, "It's a great opportunity. I'm tired of people who think we should leave this job to someone else."

Dad grilled steaks. Mom talked about the virtues of responsibility and hard work. She said things like, "Just promise me, Samuel, you won't do anything stupid." After dinner, Mac grabbed a soccer ball, and we took turns playing one-on-one with Sam until it was dark.

Sam never came home. As soon as he could, he went to jumper school.

I go back to my desk and the newspaper with the missing obituary. The hole in the paper is the size of my fist. I don't want to think about it.

Instead, I reach into my desk for my blue notebook, stuffed with Sam's letters and e-mails, printed on white paper. The newest one is on top.

Hey buddy,

Hope you are having a great tryout. Play tough!
Don't let Mischelotti eat you up. When you're
in there, channel Wayne Timcoe! Picture him
jumping up and saving that last shot.
How is school?

Last week, I had one of the best days ever. I
had the day off, so I got together with this guy
who used to jump and we went to the river to
have some fun and catch some fish. (You can
tell Dad I caught some pretty nice catfish. But
don't tell Mom I forgot my sunscreen and my

shoulders still look nasty.) Today, a bunch of us are taking an extra practice jump. We're heading to a tight spot that is surrounded by hazards. If you miss, you can guarantee yourself a medical evacuation. Wish me luck! Miss you lots! Thanks for the latest package, especially the cheese crackers. Some of the guys here never get anything. Send another when you can.

Remember: Fight to the end for what's important to you.

Happy New Year,
Sam

I send a care package to Sam and the Region Five Smokejumpers every three or four weeks. It was Steve the Sports Guy's idea.

Although he has never actually played on a team, Steve hosts a radio show, analyzes sports, and for the last year, answers manly questions with manly answers. He also has a great sense of humor. Once a month, he gets serious and devotes a column to "the right thing to do." Two months after Sam started training, Steve suggested "Things We Should Do for Our Troops."

Number one: Send supplies.

The next day, I made a list: chocolate, ramen noodles,

dried papaya, and Cheez Whiz—things everyone likes, but no one ever asks for. I put out a big box at the market. I found a picture of Sam and the logo for the Region Five Smokejumpers and taped it to a poster.

HELP LOCAL FIREFIGHTER!

The box filled up fast.

My goal is to send at least eighteen packages before my bar mitzvah, which is not a random goal.

Eighteen is the most important Jewish number. It means life. It is a good-luck number. Mom says for my bar mitzvah, I will get a lot of checks and gift cards in multiples of eighteen. Rabbi says that I'm doing a mitzvah, an obligation. He says, "You should talk about it in your speech."

Today Steve the Sports Guy writes to someone called Down the Tubes, who supports the N.Y. Jets and the Knicks and the Mets, and if that isn't depressing enough, he cannot find a good job, even though he is overqualified. He complains, "My girlfriend is impatient. I have the worst situation in the universe."

If I were Steve, I would tell Down the Tubes to stop acting like a wuss. The Jets are good. And the Knicks and the Mets . . . well . . . before the U.S. men's soccer team beat Spain, they were the butt of every World Cup joke. Good fans stick with their teams even when they stink.

But Steve does not say that. He writes: "Think positive. Do something nice for yourself. Everyone in this world has something going for them. And everyone in this world will have to face hard times. For all of us, things are good; then other times, we struggle. Your luck will change. It has to!"

If I understand correctly, he is saying: Luck is a cycle, like the economy or the number of Democrats versus Republicans in the Senate, or the sine wave we learn about in math class. Sometimes your luck goes up. Sometimes it goes down.

Sometimes it crashes down.

It's an interesting concept.

FOUR

"A man is known by the company he keeps, and also by the company from which he is kept out."

—Grover Cleveland

"Ari, can I come in?"

Now that I am twelve, Dad knocks first. This is supposed to be a privilege, but in reality, it is a formality, because he never actually waits for me to say "yes" or "no" or "hold on for a minute, I'm in the middle of something." He simply knocks, pauses, peeks, and walks into the corner of the room.

It's sort of annoying, but I have nothing to hide.

"Hey champ. I need to get going. Dave's farmers' market called—the last of the good tomatoes are in, and he cut me some chops. Why don't you call Mac and get a milkshake?" He hands me a five and pats my back. "You do understand that the late paper did not cause you to have a bad day."

I could also walk into town and check the donations box. Or write an e-mail to Sam. I sigh. "I don't know." On all counts.

The light blue paperback pamphlet from Temple Emanu-El sits on the top of a pile of books. This is my bar mitzvah notebook. It contains the blessings of the Torah and all the readings I am going to learn. The most important and hardest reading is the Torah reading. Mine comes from a section called Naso. We chose it because the rabbi said it was one of the best.

But I think he says that about all the portions, because as far as I can tell, Naso is not all that exciting. It is mostly a census—a head count of all the people in the Sinai Desert. In the chapter, God tells Moses a lot of things, but the rabbi wants me to think about one particular line about some people who are instructed to carry a Tabernacle—a sort of portable shrine—probably heavy. I have no idea what I'm supposed to actually think or say about this Tabernacle, but the rabbi says to give it time. He says it's a very significant moment, and if I work hard, I will understand everything and my speech will be great. Just in case, he gave me ten fat books full of Hebrew words, very small print, and not a whole lot of pictures.

I should probably open some of them. But the truth is prayers can't help me now.

The phone rings. If it's Coach, it will be bad news. If it's Mac, he'll want to talk about the scrimmage. He will relive every approach and every pass, forgetting, of course, that he scored those beauties on me.

Dad asks, "Don't you want to answer it?"

"No." I crumple up a shiny store circular and miss the garbage can by a mile. "Just let it ring."

In the local section, a picture of two kids fighting for control of a soccer ball takes up most of page eighteen. *With soccer season comes healthy competition between friends and busy schedules for moms.*

Dads says, "Okay then. I give up. Do what you want. See you in a few." The phone rings a second time. And two minutes after that, it rings again. This time, it does not stop. It rings and rings and rings. "Hello?" I might as well face the music.

"Fish, is that you?" A deep voice.

I knew it. "Coach?"

"We need to talk about your performance today. If that's what you want to call it."

"I'm sorry, Coach. I know I can do better. If you just give me a chance, I know I can—"

"Stop." I hear a thud. And laughter. "Fish, you idiot," Mac says, "I can't believe you fell for that."

I can't believe I fell for it either.

"Want to go out?"

"No, I don't want to go out." I sigh loud and long, so Mac knows his prank wasn't all that funny.

"Why not?"

"What do you mean, why not? I have to keep the line open. Coach really is going to call."

"He's not going to call you now. It's only been an hour."

For just one day, I'd like to be Mac. For just one day, I'd

like to be sure that I was going to get exactly what I want.

He says, "I know you don't believe me, but you are in. You looked strong. You caught a lot of tough balls. Like that one right before we took a break? That was awesome." For a moment, I feel better. Mac would tell me if he thought I stunk.

This is what most people don't get about him. On the surface, Mac and I may seem like the last two people destined to be friends. But we are friends like me and Sam are brothers. I know Mac talks in his sleep. He knows my bottom teeth are fake. In the clutch, on and off the field, we stick together. He wouldn't lie.

He says, "I mean, maybe you need some work on that move to the right, and you are a little stiff when I'm driving downfield, but it's a big net and you'll never have to face the likes of me in an actual game."

Now I feel worse. "She was good, Mac."

"She's a girl, Fish. And this is Division One. Coach may give her a spot on the team for political reasons. He may even let her play. But there's no way he'd ever start her over you. She's too short. She's too green. Biggs would eat worms before he played with her. She's just not ready."

Then he makes his voice low. "If you don't believe me, why don't you check your cosmic future . . . it is there . . . in the stars." Then he cracks up. Mac thinks the horoscopes are made up, and that I'm way too superstitious.

President Ronald Reagan, credited for a good economy and the end of the Cold War, read his horoscope every day.

I look for Pisces. Reluctantly. If I don't read it first thing in the morning, it doesn't really matter, unless . . .

Wow.

I don't believe it.

I read: "Harnessing the cosmic confidence of Mercury in Virgo can give you the extra oomph you need to shine and begin this quarter on a very positive note. You have a plan to get things moving that will bring security and prosperity to your home." I almost stand up and jump on my bed.

Mac congratulates me. "Now will you relax?"

"Yes. No. Stop making fun of me." *Extra oomph. Security and prosperity.* It's a good horoscope.

"What does mine say?" Mac's sign is Aries the Ram; an extremely confident symbol, of course.

"It says: You are a lousy, no-good friend, and in the end—"

"You're joking." For a second, he sounds hurt.

That makes me laugh. "It says: You are a natural leader, and you excel at lots of different activities. But if you're not careful, you will quickly overload. For a while, consider focusing your energy. Take a break. Try handing the reins to a trusted friend."

Mac does not waste a beat. "Focus my energy? A trusted friend? If I do that, the whole team will fall apart."

I ignore the implications of this statement and eat another cookie—this time, chocolate side first. Mac says, "So now that you know success is in your grasp, can we please go out and do something?"

The money sits on my desk. My parents won't be home for a couple of hours. If Coach decides to bench me, he can leave a message on the machine.

I tell him to meet me outside in thirty-six seconds. "Let's go to town. If I'm in for a lucky day, there is one thing I have to do."

FIVE

"Buy cards?" Mac groans. "Why don't we go to the bowling alley and get French fries instead?"

It's an eight-minute walk from our neighborhood to the blue and white awning of Ben Elliot's Hobby Emporium. Mac complains the entire time.

Although he still keeps a short stack in his top drawer, he officially stopped collecting All-Star World Soccer League cards two years ago. "Those cards are a waste of money. No one cares about them anymore."

"I care. They're—"

"I know. I know. Someday they're going to be really valuable. They're going to change your life. You've got a million of them."

"But I don't have a Timcoe."

Mac kicks a rock off the sidewalk and it hits a tree. "No offense, but no one's that lucky."

"No offense" means *You are an idiot.*

Statistically, he's right. Wayne Timcoe's trading card

is seriously rare. According to www.ussoccerfanatic.org, there were only ever 2,000 total in circulation. I've already bought twenty, thirty, forty packs—I have no idea how many. "But today is my lucky day."

We stand outside Ben Elliot's Hobby Emporium window to marvel at the display.

Ben Elliot's is easily the greatest store in Somerset Valley. Besides the usual card store inventory, they sell whoopee cushions and magic kits, fake plastic food, and real candy, like watermelon gum, that you can't get any other place. I bought my first train, my first model dinosaur, and my first trading card here. Mr. Elliot is an avid collector too, and he makes sure a train is always running around the perimeter of the store.

On sale today, for a short time only: a large white toilet that sorts coins. A vintage ship in a bottle. I say, "If you are going to make fun of me, you can wait outside."

Mac opens the door. "Well, as long as I'm here."

The front bell plays "Hava Nagillah." Mrs. Elliot sits behind the counter knitting. "Hey there, Ari. *Hag Sameach*. Any word from your brother?" She stabs her blue and yellow project with the needles, comes to the other side of the counter, and gives me a smothering hug.

"Not since last week."

"Well, I'm sure you'll hear from him soon."

"I'll tell him you said hi." Sam tries to call home on Mondays, unless he's in the field, and then he calls when he can.

I've known Mrs. Elliot since she was Miss Laura, my preschool teacher. When she sees me at Temple, she always comments on how tall I am. And that my curly hair is wasted on a boy. And that she will never forget the day I threw up in her lap.

"Go check out aisle three. Mr. Elliot found a new book about America's dirtiest presidential campaigns."

Tempting, but it can wait. Mac says, "Actually, he wants more soccer cards."

She returns to her knitting. "I hope there are some left. Mr. Elliot says you're the only one who ever buys them and from now on, you can get them on the Internet like everyone else."

We run to the back of the store.

Next to Pokémon and baseball, there they are—official All-Star World Soccer cards—three packs. One green, one blue, and one classic red. I pick them all, then put one down, then trade one for another. I have two dollars plus Dad's five—enough for two packs, but not three. Or one and a milkshake. *Wayne Timcoe, Wayne Timcoe, where are you?*

Red, blue, green.

Red, blue, green.

I hold all three colors in front of Mac. "What do you think?"

Mac turns his cap backward. "I think we should go bowling."

I put the red one back. Then I take it back and lose the green. But that doesn't feel right either, so I change my mind again, and reject the blue. Mac picks it up and takes the green pack out of my hands. "Whatever you do, get the blue. It's my favorite color. Can we go?" He grabs a plastic cockroach and we put them on the counter.

Mrs. Elliot rings me up. "That's six ninety-nine. With the roach."

I give her the money, put the penny in the give-a-penny/take-a-penny jar. "There's one pack left. Will you hold it until next week?"

When she walks down the aisle, her sneakers squeak. "Ari Fish, after all this time, are you still wishing for a . . . what's his name?"

"Timcoe."

She snatches the green pack off the shelf, throws it overhand down the aisle, and it hits my palm hard. Unbelievably hard. "It's yours. You've always been such a nice boy. If you find him, maybe you can talk about that at your bar mitzvah!"

Everyone wants to talk about my bar mitzvah, except me. "Maybe!" We run out the door to the bench outside the bookstore.

I shuffle the packs while Mac mimics Mrs. Elliot. "You really are such a nice boy. Such nice hair. And eyes." He plays with the rim of his cap. "Come on. Get it over with. Let's see what you've got."

I open the red one first. It's a good one—full of some

of my favorites. A new Michael Ballack, wearing his usual number 13, and a Day-Glo Ronaldo kicks a goal for Brazil. But there's no Timcoe. Mac grabs the Ballack. He knows I have two already.

I hand him the blue pack. "Here, you wanted it. You do it."

Mac rips the foil in his teeth. He pops the pink gum into his mouth. Then he spits it out. "Stale."

"It's always stale."

"But it should be fresh."

On the top of the pack, there is a vintage Mark "Sparky" Hughes, from when he played forward with Manchester United—the first time. Even Mac has to admit—he is extremely awesome.

But the rest of the cards are junk. Mostly second-stringers—players like me, who sit most of their careers on the bench waiting for someone to quit or get hurt.

I put Sparky to one side.

Mac waves to a girl with long brown hair. She says, "Hi. How's it going?" And he asks, "Hey, Becky. What's the word?" He gets up to walk her to the corner. She looks like a lot of girls when they talk to Mac—extremely happy and nervous.

All the girls in our class think Mac is cute. They call him on the phone, just to talk. They think he looks like a movie star. The only time they call me is to find out who he likes.

That's easy to tell. When Mac talks to a girl he thinks

is cute, he keeps his hands in his pockets. He shifts his weight from his left to his right. He looks up at the sky or ceiling and smiles so she can get a good look at the dimple on his chin. I don't know where or when he learned how to do this, but it is extremely effective. Even though his jokes are dumb, the girl always laughs.

Right now, Becky laughs.

He looks at the sky and grins until her ride comes.

I hold the last pack, the green one, rub it between my palms. The corner is torn just slightly. The lettering on the foil looks faded. Mac is right. Finding Wayne would be like finding a pearl in a swimming pool. And even if I uncover someone great, I cannot change what happened. Magic isn't going to make my life better. If I have to, I'll play another season at backup. Or maybe I should call the coach of the Super Two team. My horoscope was my horoscope even before I read it, and still, on the field, I stunk.

The Super Two is not the worst league in the world.

Mac sprints back, just before the Will's Beverage truck rumbles toward the intersection. We pump fists. "Beer Man." The truck bounces over a frost heave and speeds through the yellow light.

Mac says, "That's my third sighting this week."

"You are so lucky." Will's Beverage truck is the coolest thing on four wheels, even better than a Hummer, or Mrs. Mac's last boyfriend's vintage Beetle bus. The truck is jet black with bright red lettering, and the chrome on the oversized tires is painted yellow. The horn sounds like a ship's; the engine is loud.

Beer Man wears mirrored aviator sunglasses and a Red Sox cap, even when it's cloudy. According to Sam, Will used to drive the truck himself. He claims that the first Beer Man to take over was Coach, but Coach swears that's only a rumor.

"So, what are you waiting for?" Mac asks. "Isn't this supposed to be your lucky day?"

I tear open the green foil. Mac looks over my shoulder. I reveal the first card. Mac grabs it out of my hand. "Hey. Check that out. Clint Dempsey."

Mac loves Dempsey. In seventy-one games with the Revolution, he scored twenty-five goals.

We put him in the "keep" pile. The next two cards are excellent too.

Mac asks, "Who is Marcello Lippi? Have you ever heard of Lev Yashin?"

Sometimes I don't know how Mac calls himself a soccer fan. Lippi was the manager who benched Roberto Baggio. Love him or hate him, it was a bold move. And Yashin was the best goalkeeper to ever play the game—and that's not just my opinion—he was on FIFA's twentieth-century dream team. The guy was from Russia and had some of the best reflexes I have ever seen. I've got three Yashin cards at home. I will send this one to Sam.

"You know, I think this one is rare." Mac grabs the

Lippi, and the rest of the pack flutters to the ground. I drop to my knees to pick them up fast. I don't want any of them to get dirty. Or wet.

That's when I see it.

Third card from the bottom. A flash of blue. As in Revolution blue. With a vibrant red Revolution stripe.

Sun shining on a green field near Boston.

It is too perfect. Too predictable. *You will succeed.*

I know before I see him, before Mac starts screaming, before he starts jumping up and down like we just won Olympic gold.

Wayne Timcoe, my hero, my brother's hero, is crouched on one knee, in front of a large white net.

It's Wayne—Wayne Timcoe—smiling at the camera. He was the greatest player to ever come off a Somerset Valley field.

Mine.

SIX

"You've got to learn to survive a defeat. That's when you develop character."

—Richard Nixon

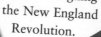

Wayne Timcoe:
(1974–)

Wayne Timcoe was born in Somerset Valley, Massachusetts, to Bethany and Craig Timcoe, an NCAA Division Two referee. The fourth of seven boys, Wayne displayed an uncanny ability to stop, catch, and throw a soccer ball as early as age three. At nine, he was the youngest boy to ever play goalkeeper on the National Junior team. He was the anchor of three high school and two state championships, before signing with the New England Revolution.

REVOLUTION

The picture was taken at the beginning of his rookie season. It's the same one from *The Ultimate Year Book*.

The bio only tells part of his story.

After Wayne Timcoe graduated from Somerset Valley High and signed that contract, the town threw him a parade. I was a baby. Sam was younger than I am now. Dad took a picture of us, Sam cradling me in front of the newly painted billboard over the scoreboard: Home of Wayne Timcoe.

It's still one of my favorite screen savers.

The first stories I remember are all about Wayne. Sam loved to talk about him. "He had the biggest, best hands I've ever seen. He could anticipate a shot, like he knew where the ball was going—like he was inside the kicker's head. Once, I saw him stop three penalty kicks in a row. No lie."

But the big leagues test you. In his fourth game of his rookie season, Wayne injured his ankle—a complex sprain. It was so complex that he never made it back to the field that season. The following year, he injured the other ankle twice. They sent him down; they brought him up. He would walk on the field, just to hobble off. The critics started saying "washout."

Loser.

All promise. No play.

Beyond unlucky.

Sam swears he knew that Wayne was the kind of guy who needed adversity to get him motivated. He said, "Those announcers thought they knew everything. But they didn't know Wayne."

Since then, I've read tons of articles about Wayne's

third season. Most of them cite that this was the year Wayne Timcoe "learned the system." Although I am not sure what "the system" means when it comes to defending an open net, I do know he started fifteen consecutive games. He finished with an eight and seven record. The cynics named him Most Improved Player of the league.

Sports Illustrated made him their cover story, the week of April 22. That issue is wrapped in plastic in my bottom drawer.

His fourth year was huge. I've studied every one of his games on tape, and I know for a fact, the guy was in the zone. You can see it even on the small screen. He recorded three straight shutouts, and took his team all the way to the finals. It was the first year Sam started for the high school team. We had a party to watch the big game.

I have to admit, I don't remember actually seeing Wayne Timcoe save the game-deciding shot, pounding his fists in the air, although my dad has told me that right after that play, I put on my Superman cape, stood on a coffee table, and told everyone I would be the next great goalkeeper. And everybody cheered.

Since that day, I've watched what happened next at least a thousand times.

The scene starts out funny, men laughing and crying and jumping on top of each other after the clock ticks to zero. They are all so happy. They hug each other and rip off their shirts and pile up like we do in the backyard.

The mood changes fast. First, a few guys step back. They start waving people over. Another runs for help. Someone else puts his head in his hands. It is clear something is wrong. When the pile empties, only one blue and red jersey stays down.

Crumpled.

Face down.

The only movement: one thumb up.

Under that pile of men, Wayne Timcoe was trampled by his own teammates. They immobilized his neck, put him on a board, and took him off the field on a stretcher. In one celebration, his career went from perfect to bleak, his game went from dominating to back on hold.

But lots of guys get injured. And a lot of them come back. Bad luck is supposed to make you stronger. Adversity turns to grit. A torn Achilles tendon is not supposed to end your career. One concussion is not the end of the world.

Sam and I followed every operation and report. There were three surgeries, two for infection. He went to rehab. We paid attention to every rumor—from sightings of Wayne Timcoe in the gym, to reports of his taking drills on the field. He was lifting. He was running. He was going to parties in New York and Los Angeles with some singer.

First he was going to play in England. Then Italy. Then he announced he was taking a little time off to regroup. We were sure this was just a ploy. He was Wayne Timcoe. He was mounting the most amazing comeback the soccer world had ever known.

But that never happened. The articles stopped. He disappeared from soccer, from Somerset Valley, from the planet. Soccer found new goalkeepers. The World Cup came and went and came again. The league did not reissue his card. Soon there weren't a whole lot of people who still cared about Wayne.

But I still believed. So did Sam. So did Mac. We began collecting cards. We sat on my bed and created fantasy teams and talked about who was the best of each season, decade, and century.

We still hoped that somehow, he would come back to the game.

By then, I was playing four days a week. Sam became a firefighter. The day after his first big jump, he told me jumping out of a plane was even better than scoring the winning goal. "You're the soccer star now," he said. "Move the poster to your room. For good luck."

"Are you sure?" I asked. "He's your hero."

"He's our hero," Sam said. "And he always will be." We relived that last save and even a few of Sam's greatest goals. He said, "Remember, fight to the end for what is important to you."

Wayne said that before every big game.

Now Mac stares at the card. He stares at me. I pinch him. He pinches me. We cannot stop screaming and laughing. He says, "I don't believe it. I absolutely, positively don't believe you found him."

Somehow I manage to secure the card in my pocket. Somehow I manage not to throw up. Somehow I run faster than Mac all the way to our neighborhood and my house. I go straight up the stairs, three at a time, to my room. I look at our Wayne Timcoe poster, the card, the poster, the card.

I bend my knees.

I picture the ball.

I hear the cheers. For me. I hear people cheering for me. Sam was right—when you want something bad enough, anything can happen.

Anything.

You can break your leg.

You can jump out of a plane into a fire.

You can find the lucky card you've been looking for.

Coach calls after dinner. He asks me how my classes are going. "You feeling good about your work?"

I do.

He is glad. "Well, I'm calling to tell you I've made my decision, and you are my guy. You are going to start in the net." His voice sounds a bit slow, so I check the Caller ID, just to make sure it is really him.

It is. It is really him. He is really telling me that I am the starter. And Mac is the captain. Everything we wanted is coming true right now.

"We play most Saturdays. Sometimes Wednesdays too. Mandatory practice every weekday but Monday. No excuses."

Some way, somehow, I manage to maintain enough self-control not to drop to my knees and cry. My voice does not even shake. "Thank you for this opportunity. Is there anything in particular I should know about Greenview?"

"Focus on their center. The guy has shifty moves, but don't panic—he's all they have. He's at his best when he's in the corners. Remember last year, he stung Mischelotti with three corner kicks, and knocked us right out of contention."

I remember that loss. "But last year, Eddie never played the post. Mischelotti thought he could do it himself. We left too many offensive players unguarded."

Coach likes the way I think. The last thing he says: "Now that you're the keeper, you tell them where to stand."

I put down the phone in shock. I'm the keeper.

I'm going to tell them.

I am the happiest person in the universe.

From downstairs, Dad yells, "Ari, are you still on the phone? Your mother says you need to practice your Hebrew."

I yell back, "Don't worry. The starting keeper will get the job done," and before I can say *Baruch Atah Adonai*, which are the first three words of every blessing in the

Jewish universe, he is upstairs and he is jumping on me, and then he asks me if I'm okay, because he has just tackled me, and Wayne Timcoe, the poster, is looking down on us.

After one cookie, a piece of cake, two peaches, and a plum, my dad finally calls it a celebration. I e-mail samthefish@reddingfive.com.

> Hi Sam. E-mail me as soon as you can. Or call.
> NOW. Now would be good. Something amazing
> just happened!!! You are not going to believe it!!!

I can't wait to tell him, "I did it! I am the starting keeper. I have a Timcoe. A real Timcoe. I am the luckiest person in Somerset Valley. My season is going to be great."

SEVEN

"To be prepared for war is one of the most effectual means of preserving peace."

—George Washington

There are a lot of theories about luck.

Luck is no more than believing you are lucky. Luck happens when preparation meets opportunity. It is what is left over after you give one hundred percent.

But this is what I think: Sometimes there is no explanation. Good luck is good luck.

Look at me. Now that I have Wayne, I am living proof.

For example, although the weatherman declared that the steady rain would probably continue for at least five more days, the morning after I find Wayne Timcoe, a cold front changes direction and the sun begins to shine. The grass dries up. Even though Indian summer usually means my allergies are a mess, my nose does not run.

For four straight days, my game improves. I make diving saves and punching saves. My throws are strong, and my kicks are more accurate than they ever were when there was no card. When I make a mistake, I don't get stressed out. Instead, I talk to Coach. I figure out what I have to change so that I won't do it again.

Coach says, "Ari, I love this new attitude." He says, "The position of goalkeeper is the most important to the team!" He reminds me that I have to think ahead, that the best keepers command the defense. I have to get used to seeing the entire field, so I can properly distribute the ball, once I've stopped it.

I remind him that Wayne Timcoe once lost a game because he got rid of the ball too fast. "I will not lose my cool in the heat of the moment."

He smiles. "Okay, young man, why don't we test that promise?"

Coach lines everyone up in front of the net into two teams. He grabs Mac and Parker and gives each of them ten balls. Their job: to alternate their shots in speed, placement, and distance. My job: to stop as many as possible.

It is an extremely hard drill.

But today I can do it. I stop four of Mac's shots and all but two of Parker's.

Mac looks like he wants to call it a day, but Parker sets up for another round, which makes Coach very happy. He tells her that if she keeps doing what she's doing, he will definitely put her in position to score.

Mac nearly has a conniption. "Soup and I don't need help on our line." He points to this new kid, named David Young, who has already been dubbed David Old.

"If we get jammed, Old can move up. He's stronger than she is."

That might be true, but right now, Coach makes it clear he wants to leave all his options open. He congratulates Parker. "In just a short amount of time, you have really taken it up a notch." He gives her an extra turn around the cones. And when she scores on me, even I have to admit she is a very wily player.

In the morning, on our way to school, Mac is still stewing.

"She is too short.

"She never heads the ball.

"She smiles all the time."

Tomorrow is our first game. I am not completely comfortable making fun of her behind her back. "Lay off her, Mac. You can't fault her for everything."

"Yes, I can. She is so annoying. And don't tell me you don't think it's weird that every time Coach needs a volunteer, she raises her hand and smiles like she can't wait to do another stupid job."

He forgets that last year, we raised our hands every time Coach needed something. "Mac, give her a break. She's a backup. You don't even know if Coach will play her." When he starts to argue and sulk, I say, "You have to admit, no one will expect her to be good. The focus will still be on you."

That makes him smile. "You think?"

"I think."

"It's still bad." He walks faster. "The entire town is laughing at us. Do you see how shiny her cleats are? She must clean them every night."

I clean my cleats after every practice. "But they'll stop laughing when you break Sam's record for goals in a single season . . . when the offense rolls, even with a girl." When he doesn't relax, I take out Wayne. "It's destiny," I say. "Everything is going to go our way."

We make fists and pound high and low, then shake in two directions. I remind him that Wayne has to stay a secret.

"Please don't tell anyone," I say.

"Tell anyone what?" Over the years, we have kept a lot of secrets, some almost as big as this one.

"Seriously, I have a strong feeling about this. I don't think anyone should know about him but you and me and Sam."

When I say seriously, I mean it. Mac knows it's important.

He picks up handfuls of gravel and pelts trees. *Ping, ping, ping.* He hits a mailbox three times out of three. "This morning, I heard there was this mega-fire near San Francisco. Was Sam in it? Do you think he's seen any burned people?"

Ping.

Ping.

I put the card away. "He doesn't say."

The San Francisco fire must be new. Across the state,

they are down to one hundred and eleven fires. Most are contained. Sam must be in one of them, because he has not answered my e-mail.

Mac says, "I wonder if he gets to pull a lot of good-looking girls out of burning houses."

Miss.

In his letters, Sam sticks to neutral stuff like hi/how are you/what's happening? On the phone, he tells me that he never gets tired of jumping out of a plane and how much he loves floating in the sky. That when his parachute opens up, he feels pure joy. He also tells me that even though no one knows his name, the people are so happy to see the smokejumpers, they make posters and hang them all over town. He always says, "This season is so crazy. Don't worry if you don't hear from me. I could be out for days at a time."

There's no blood. No death. If it's scary, he doesn't say. And I don't ask. I never ask. Too many specifics lead to too much thinking. Sam has never been in trouble. He can do whatever he sets out to do.

Mac wants to know every gory detail. "What if they're dead? Does he have to touch those people too? Does he get to stuff them in body bags?"

We cross the street in front of our school. I know Mac is just curious, but I wish he would stop asking. I have one practice before my first big game. I do not want to talk about my brother or fire or even Parker. I yell, "Last one to the double door buys ice cream."

We run side by side down the path. Right then left, up the small hill, and down the winding path toward the main entrance of our school. He passes the flagpole just before me, but I pull ahead halfway up the front steps. Normally, this is where he loses me. Normally, this is where I give up.

But not today.

Today, he doesn't lose me. I don't give up. I almost believe in magic.

Today, for the first time ever, I win. Easy.

EIGHT

"The capacity of the female mind for studies of the highest order cannot be doubted, having been sufficiently illustrated by its works of genius, of erudition, and of science."

—James Madison

In the hall, two girls wave. They say, "Hey, Ari," which means they are talking to me, and they know my name. For the fifth day in a row, I don't trip. In social studies, Eddie remembers to save my seat. We start a unit on the Civil War, the bloodiest war in American history, one of my five favorite topics after the presidents.

Mr. Sigley hands each of us a pretest. Usually, at the start of a new unit, I don't know any of the answers.

What was the first major battle of the Civil War?

In what campaign did Grant sustain 50,000 casualties?

When did Lee surrender?

Today, they're cake. I know them all. *Bull Run; the Wilderness campaign; April 9, 1865.*

I raise my hand. "Did you know that the war began as

the result of a dispute between certain Southern states and certain Northern states regarding slavery and the taxation of cotton exports?"

Mr. Sigley says, "That's very interesting, Ari. You really know a lot about the Civil War. Please feel free to chime in anytime."

Participation is worth forty percent of our grade. After class, I can't stop smiling.

Eddie says, "I can't believe you know all that!" Then he asks me if I want a ride to the field—his mom is picking him up.

"That sounds great." As we walk to our next class, I pull a crumpled five-dollar bill out of my back pocket that I forgot was there. I envision the Wayne Timcoe card safe in my backpack. Everything keeps getting better, and I don't think it's a coincidence.

In math, I figure out the answer to the problem of the day.

In English, the book we are reading next has very short chapters. When the teacher gives the assignment, I know exactly what to write.

At lunch, the whole team sits together at the two tables in the middle of the room. Becky comes over with Sandy, the striker from the girls' club team, and Randi and Kellie, whom I have never seen break a sweat, even though they were in my gym class for two years straight. They ask if they can squeeze in too. According to Sandy, Parker has been bragging all week about how great and nice we all are. Randi and Kellie offer to make signs for every Somerset Valley soccer game and put them all over the school. No one has ever done this for a club soccer team before. They write down all our names, so they won't spell any of them wrong.

"Fish," I say, "as in gold."

And they laugh. Their brown ponytails swing together.

Pretty soon, they're all sketching and comparing notes and trading papers. As far as I can tell, the point is to incorporate the letters of each name into a big picture or design.

They finish Eddie's name first, because names with double letter combinations are way cooler and fun than names with a variety of letters, and Eddie has two sets. I see what they mean. The g's in *Biggs* look especially good next to each other, and the girls decorate them with a lot of squares and swirls and colors.

Becky makes Mac's, complete with golden arches, and the ball flying right over the top, which of course, Mac loves. He looks at the ceiling and tells a joke. Soup gets a can of soup with the slogan: "Mmm. He's good."

Sandy hands it to Soup. "Do you like it?"

When Soup blushes, his dark skin looks almost purple. "Yes. I do." Soup never says much. He might be confident on the field, but lately, he has become extremely shy, especially around girls. Mac thinks this has something to do with his family or culture, but I think it's because his voice is changing. At least, it's gotten a lot lower a lot faster than mine or Mac's. And he is the first person to get hair over his lip. I wouldn't have noticed, except Soup is constantly touching it when he thinks no one is looking.

Next, they start working on mine. They experiment turning the dots over the *i*'s into stars. Then the end of the *h* becomes a tidal wave and they change their minds and turn the *i*'s into bubbles. "We can draw a shark too. Eating a soccer ball. That will be cool." The shark has an open mouth, revealing long, sharp teeth.

It looks excellent. I still wish I had a cooler sounding name, like Tiger or River or Darius or Lance, a name that made me sound more electric and less like someone destined to study math. Something with a good nickname. Like Ike. Or Jimmy. Or Jack. Millard Fillmore, our thirteenth president, had the worst nickname in the history of the presidents—the American Louis Philippe.

He was only elected once.

Parker squeezes in next to me just as they finish the shark. The girls ask her if she wants to be Parker, Parks, or just P, and she shakes her head. "You don't have to make one for me," she says. "Wait until I'm starting."

They all protest way too loud. "We are not waiting. You make soccer history. You get a sign."

Girls can be so melodramatic.

They draw. I open my lunch. There's a sandwich, two black and white cookies, a bag of carrots, and some fruit. I stare at it, because I don't want to look at Parker. I would feel the same way she does. It is never easy being a backup.

The girls make Parker's sign. It shows Parker in Supergirl clothes, kicking a giant ball.

She looks a little happier. "Thanks, guys." Then she admires the rest of the signs. When she sees mine, Parker says, "My father told me that Ari is a Hebrew word for lion. If you don't like the shark, a lion would make a great poster too."

Mac takes one of my cookies. "Are you crazy? Do not call Fish a lion. The lion is the king. As in the top dog. He can't call himself that. He'll look like a goon."

I have to agree. "Really, the shark is enough."

Parker opens her bag and takes out a turkey sandwich, chips, and a black and white cookie, the same as mine. "I don't know. It might be fun if people called you the Lion. Because you were really ferocious this week. We were hitting some beastly shots and you didn't seem to be bothered at all. You really are playing great."

Ferocious.

Beastly.

My entire defense cracks up laughing. Later on, I bet Mac'll say Parker is pathetic for trying to be nice.

I take a big bite of cookie. At exactly the same moment, Parker bites hers too. We both eat the white side first. Mac passes me a note, on a torn piece of notebook paper. It says: "Let's get out of here now." When I don't respond, he writes another one: "Can't you eat faster?"

Parker acts like she doesn't see us passing notes. "I think everyone should eat dessert first. It seems so standard not to. Why do we always save the best for last?" When I don't have anything to say but "yes, I agree," she starts telling me a story about when her dad played soccer. According to her, he was pretty good. Even played in college. As she talks, she waves her hands and shakes her ponytail. And her eyelashes flutter, like she's got something in her eye.

When she finally takes another bite of cookie, I tell her a story about the season Sam broke the select scoring record. When I am finished, Mac kicks me under the table. Right below the knee. "Ow."

Parker picks up the bread from the top half of her sandwich. "Do you ever put potato chips inside your sandwich?" When I admit that I have never once put chips between the bread, she says, "It's really good. You want to try it?"

"Okay. I'll try." Mac kicks me again. Ow. Same spot. I take some of her chips and I have to admit, turkey sandwiches with chips are a thousand times better than turkey sandwiches flat.

Now Mac looks at me like I'm eating poison. "Not for me," he says. "I'm in training."

Parker looks at him like he smells funny. "That's too bad. Because it's really good." Then she leans in close and whispers in my ear, "He thinks he is so clever."

Mac immediately gets up. "Gotta go," he says. He smiles at Becky, and she gets up too. Soup and Eddie crumple up their lunch bags and follow. At the same time, Sandy, Randi, and Kellie scoot to the far end of the table and giggle about something, hopefully not me. I stuff most of my sandwich into my mouth, but before I can make my move, or chew, or swallow, Parker asks, "Would you wait a minute?"

We are essentially alone. This does not feel exactly like good luck. I swallow the gigantic wad of turkey, bread, and chips. It would be even better with cranberry sauce. "What do you want?"

Her eyes look sad. And a little mad. "Why won't he be nice to me?" I almost cough the whole thing right back up.

"He looks at me like I'm a criminal. Don't try and deny it."

If I have to, I'll plead the Fifth. "Just play hard. Don't be a liability. That's all Mac wants."

"Really?" She looks relieved. "Well, I can definitely do that." Then she smiles in a sneaky way. "I can't tell you what it is, but I have a secret weapon."

Now, that is funny. I'm the one with the secret weapon. It's better than anything she has. "Well, if you work hard, and if Coach decides to start you—"

"You mean *when* he decides. It's only a matter of time." Somehow, the way she looks at me, I know she wants to say something I don't want to hear. "Ari, you won't make fun of me if I ask you a question?"

"No." I really regret not leaving with Mac. "What?"

"How did you do it?"

"Do what?"

"Sit on the sidelines." She sighs. "Did you ever think about quitting? You had to know you could do the job just as well as Mischelotti."

This must be a girl thing. Even when it's true, guys never talk like this. "It is what it is. I wouldn't call it terrible. I had a job to do for the team. I had to be ready to go in. Just in case."

She does not need to know how much I hated every minute. Or that there were days I believed that the only reason Coach kept me on the team was to make sure Mac had a ride to the field. I say, "Besides, Coach practically promised you a starting position on the offense. He thinks you're great." I want to get out of here. "Last year, I didn't have that. Sometimes I played sweeper, but that was it."

She finishes her crunchy sandwich. Apologizes a few times for being so nosy. "I know I should be psyched, and I hope this doesn't bother you, but I can't totally be happy. It's my dream to start in the net."

I must look like it bothers me, because she backpedals fast. "I'm not saying I want you to get hurt like Mischelotti. And you've really taught me a lot. But I'm hoping that if we are in a blowout, or if you hit a rough patch . . ."

"I will not hit a rough patch."

She starts tearing up her plastic wrap. "No, this is coming out wrong. I don't think you will. I just want you to know I'm taking extra practice. I'm doing everything I can to be ready. Would you be upset if I asked Coach for a little more time in the net during practice? So he could see what I'm learning?"

Mac is not going to believe this. I would never have asked Mischelotti for extra time. "I thought you liked playing offense."

She balls up the shredded plastic. "I do. But it's not my favorite." She won't look at me. "Everybody has a dream."

I wish Sam were home. If he were, he would probably tell me to stand tall, that I am the starter. That I wouldn't want a backup who didn't want to play. That I will not lose my first game and I won't mess up in the net and Coach won't give the job to Parker—especially if she can score. He would quote his favorite president, FDR: "The only thing to fear is fear itself." And to him, the fear would not be insurmountable.

Those chips are hanging out in the bottom of my gut.

At practice, Coach sends Parker to midfield with Soup, David, and Eddie to do speed ladders. I tell Mac everything Parker said.

"You don't have to take that." He is furious. "Who does that girl think she is?"

I feel better already. "Does she really think Coach is going to change his mind?"

We watch her sprint across the field. She can almost keep up with Soup, which is saying a lot. Soup is fast, one of the best pure athletes on the team. Coach tells them to do it again—this time while passing the ball. Mac is not happy. He asks if he shouldn't do this with Soup instead of Parker. Coach shakes his head and sends us to the net. "Why don't you two practice some penalty kicks?"

Mac says, "Sure. No problem." He pumps his fist. I get ready for the worst. Penalty kicks favor the offense— they are almost impossible to defend. The only way I'm going to stop Mac MacDonald is if he wants me to.

Coach tells Mischelotti to sit on the far bench and give me pointers.

"Don't take it easy on him," Mischelotti tells Mac. "I know you guys are friends, but a good keeper needs to be tested."

NINE

"Character is like a tree and reputation like a shadow. The shadow is what we think of it; the tree is the real thing."

—Abraham Lincoln

Mac kicks right. I jump right.

He kicks left.

I get him again.

Left, then right. First slow. Then fast. Every time, I focus on his foot and his eye.

Mac kicks again.

"Got it."

He spits on the ground. "I don't believe it." He reties his cleats.

But that doesn't change anything. Whether he kicks left, right, or over the top—it doesn't faze me. I have found my focus. I can read him before the ball has left the ground. I stop nine out of thirteen shots, which is really unbelievable.

After two more saves, Mischelotti stops play, but it's

not to help me. "You must be flinching, MacDonald. Fish can read you a mile away."

"I am not flinching." Mac sets up, turns his foot, stares right, and kicks again. Right into my hands. In the history of me versus him, he has never had to work this hard to get a ball past me. But today, even when he tries to fake me out, I stop him cold.

I've got calluses. But my hands don't sting.

After another twenty balls, I feel like Helmuth Duckadam, the Hero of Seville, who saved four consecutive penalty shots, a first in European competition. Mac points over my head. "Look at that. The double x's are on!"

"You're kidding!" The double x in the Exxon sign has been dark for years. I whip around, but I don't get it—the sign looks the way it always does. The e and the n are on, the o blinks, and the double x is black. A few years ago, some kids threw rocks at it until it smashed.

Mac kicks one through. "Gotcha!"

The ball rolls past me, into the back of the net.

A whistle sounds, and Coach waves us to midfield. Mischelotti gets up and leans on his crutches. "Nice job, Fisherman. Mac, take the ball. You're going to have to be faster if you want to get the rock past the Greenview keeper."

Coach is not that harsh. Tomorrow is a big game. We all need to sleep well/eat well/take it easy. And of course, don't do anything that might mess up our heads.

Then he blows the whistle again. "Four laps and you're done." Before I can get going, he pulls me out of line. "You look great, Fish. Stronger every day. For the first time, you're playing like you know you're good."

He tells me not to bother running. "I want your legs fresh for tomorrow." He pats me on the back and chuckles. "This is what a coach hopes for, Ari. That someone will listen and put in the work and it will all pay off." We watch the rest of the team circle the field. "If you keep playing like this, Greenview doesn't stand a chance."

The next morning, my horoscope reads: "You might find yourself in deep water, but if you show wisdom and strength, the current won't feel so rough. Go with the flow. Look beyond the obvious. Observe the bigger picture."

This is a perfect prediction. Of course I'll be in deep water. What could be deeper than being the starting keeper in your first game?

What bigger picture can there be than an entire field?

My shower is hot and strong and my cereal stays crunchy all the way to the bottom of the bowl. I consider writing letters to both the Kellogg's and Post corporations to thank them. Never before have I eaten such an excellent and truly crunchy breakfast.

Next, I hit the floor. Fifty push-ups. Forty-four presidents. The headline today: "Army Unit Stabilizes Village. Locates Notorious Al-Qaeda Leader."

Go Army!

I put on my T-shirt, pack my cleats and an extra shirt with the rest of my gear, and double-triple-check that Wayne is still wrapped securely in Sam's last letter. To keep him safe, I put the card and the letter in a plastic bag. Then I smooth it so it is as close to airtight as a ziplock bag can be. The whole thing fits perfectly in the front pocket of my pack.

I look at the poster and say, "I am going to win this game." It feels good.

Steve the Sports Guy always says that you have to believe in yourself. He says, "Pump yourself up. Tell yourself you are the man," but I've never had the nerve to do it before.

"I am going to stop their center.

"I am going to stop their striker."

A large, black spider dangles from a string just over my desk.

"I am going to stop every corner kick." The spider freezes in space. It's instinct. She thinks I'm going to kill her.

I'm not a big fan of spiders, but I'm not stupid either. Killing that spider today would be bad luck. I turn my back so she can weave her way down to the desk and get out of here. Wayne, the poster, stares me down. I ask, "What? You don't think I'm ready? Should I do more push-ups? Recite the vice presidents just for insurance?"

"You don't need insurance."

Mom stands in the doorway, no knock from her. "Almost ready for your first game as Somerset Valley's greatest keeper ever?"

She is so corny. "Yes. I'm ready."

"Good." Mac comes upstairs, sits on the desk, and before I can say, "Don't do that," swipes the spider with the back of his hand. With the same hand, he tries to pat my back, but fortunately, I get out of the way.

No dead spider karma on me.

We run outside, load our gear, and climb into the backseat. Mom says, "Buckle up, boys."

Mac elbows me in the ribs. He likes to make fun of my mom's obsession with safety. Behind her back, he complains we'd get there a whole lot faster if his speed demon mother would drive.

Sometimes I wish she would. I wish we could ride in the back of her messy car, if just once, she could be the embarrassing mom.

But Mac's mom is not your average mom. She is a lot younger than all the other moms—and extremely pretty. Most mornings, she wears ripped jeans and a tank top without anything underneath, like she's a girl and not a lady. She's had a million boyfriends, and she never lived with Mac's dad or even knows where he is now. Mac says, "What you don't know, you don't miss," but that's what she tells him to say. The truth is when she doesn't show up to the all-school spring concert or parent meetings or even our games, he wishes she were there. Mac looks for his father too. He looks for an athletic guy. A man who looks like him or plays like him or tells jokes all the time, just like him.

When Mac comes over to drink our milk because the milk in his fridge tastes like cheese, we say nothing. I never tell him that I hear him crying in his sleep.

My parents are only too happy to take us boys wherever we need to be, and most of the time, that is fine with me. I like showing up places with Mac. Wherever we go, everyone is always happy to see him.

Once our belts are buckled, Mom pulls out of the driveway slow. She drives down the street slow. Just in case there is any chance of driving near the speed limit, she rides the brakes all the way to the corner, where she comes to a full stop, even though the street is completely empty. Before turning left onto the main street, she looks left, right, and left again.

The field is four miles away, straight down this road. After one mile, two cars are stuck behind us.

Three.

Four.

One toots.

Another wants to pass us, but now there's traffic in the opposite direction. When she stops in front of a crosswalk, the entire line of cars slam on the brakes. Mom waves the people across. The father waves "thank you" as the children run across the street. The second the street is clear, a low foghorn blares. We whip around and look out the back window. It's the jet black Will's Beverage truck, half a block back.

Fist bump. "Beer Man."

On cue, he revs up the engine.

My mother scowls. She can't stand drivers who act like their time is more important than hers. "I thought it was against the law to install a straight-pipe exhaust." She may be the slowest driver in the universe, but she has two sons. She knows her engine modifications.

When the road widens, she pulls into the right lane. Beer Man accelerates into the opposite side of the street and burns rubber.

Mac whistles. "That's my seventh sighting in ten days. It's like he's following me."

"You wish." I haven't seen him since the day I found Wayne, and even that seems like a lot.

Mom shakes her head and *tsk*s. "Jerry MacDonald, you think that man is some kind of cult hero, but mark my words. Someday he is going to hurt someone."

She can be so embarrassing. "Can't we please drive a little bit faster? I need time to warm up."

A car pulls in front of her. She leans on the brakes. "Didn't your horoscope say something about showing wisdom in deep water?"

I get it. Be quiet and stop complaining.

I say nothing when she makes a full stop before each crosswalk. I say nothing when she lets two cars pull into the empty parking lot next to the field.

Mac thanks her profusely for the ride. "My mom really appreciates it," he says. "You know how busy she is."

Mac runs ahead, but Mom makes no move to get out. "Aren't you coming?" I ask.

"Wouldn't miss it for the world," she says while she opens her cell phone. "I just need to check my messages and wait for your dad."

This sounds fishy. My mother thinks life was easier when people weren't so readily available. I ask, "Is there something you aren't telling me?"

She looks a little embarrassed. "Okay, fine. If you must know, I'm waiting for your dad to get here, so we can say a little prayer." She turns off her phone. "It's the first game. We always say a prayer when one of our sons starts for the first time."

I laugh. "You can count some presidents while you're at it." I guess I'm not the only person in the family with pregame rituals.

I get out of the car, grab my gear, and start walking. She leans out her window as Eddie's car pulls into the parking lot. "Have a great game, Division One Starting Keeper. Remember, heads up. And don't forget to wear your mouth guard."

TEN

"Confidence . . . thrives only on honesty, on honor, on the sacredness of obligation, on faithful performance. Without them, it cannot live."
—Franklin D. Roosevelt

SOMERSET VALLEY vs. GREENVIEW

SOMERSET VALLEY COMMUNITY FIELD
10 A.M. START

There are two main soccer fields in Somerset Valley. The first one belongs to the high school and is surrounded by bleachers and has lights for night games. Our field, known as the other field, has one bleacher, three rows high, and one lone elm tree, the last tree in Somerset Valley not to get hit by the Dutch elm disease. According to my dad, the town spends a lot of time and money keeping it alive.

Sam claims that Wayne actually sat under this particular elm tree doing his homework, hanging out before or after practice.

Kissing girls.

Now it is the only place with shade, the only place to tack up a sign.

So it's covered.

Go Mac! Score Big! You are the Man!

Go Parker! First Girl Ever in the Division One Select League!

There are smaller banners for every player, including Eddie, Soup, and Old. But the biggest poster is for me. *Save the day, Ari Fish!* A great white shark lunges out of a huge *h* wave, about to eat the soccer balls over the *i*'s. Tiny lions smile from every corner. It's the nicest, most colorful poster of all.

I follow Mac to the far end of the bleachers, away from the tree and the signs and the rest of our friends. "Maybe we should go sit somewhere else?" I assume he wants to see Wayne.

"Why? What are you talking about?" He sounds mad, even though Parker is nowhere to be seen.

I hit him in the shoulder. "I thought you wanted to see Wayne Timcoe. Why else would you sit all the way over here?"

Mac shrugs his shoulders, and stretches his hamstrings for two and a half seconds each, which really is not enough to make any kind of difference. "Sure, why not? I guess it can't hurt."

We grab my bag and head over to the Porta-Pottys, adorned by red, white, and blue streamers and a bouquet of wilted balloons. The air smells like ammonia. I take the plastic bag out of my backpack and unfold Sam's letter carefully. He tries to grab it. "What's that?"

"A letter from Sam." I hold it out of reach.

"Cool. Can I read it?" He goes for it again like he has a right, like Sam is his brother too, like one letter is more exciting than my lucky Wayne Timcoe card. "Please? He hasn't written me in ages."

"This one is private," I say, even though it isn't.

Mac tries to grab it out of my hands. He almost rips it. Somehow I manage to shove it into my pack, unharmed. Now he definitely looks mad. "Just tell me, does he tell you to fight to the end for what is big?"

"For what's important."

I hand him the card. "Here. Rub it against your leg. I've been doing that every morning, and it's been giving me great luck."

"You rub it on your leg?" Mac looks at me, then the card. He gives it back, no rub, no thank you. "That is the weirdest thing I've ever heard."

"What's weird?" Parker walks out of a Porta-Potty.

"Nothing."

I sit on the card and hope Mac will just let her walk away.

She stands in front of us and plays with her braid. "Come on, tell me."

"It's just guy stuff," Mac says. "Nothing that you need to know about."

Parker sticks out her tongue, and he does too. She jogs to the field. She turns around and says, "I'll show you, Mac MacDonald."

Mac isn't fazed one bit. "Oooh, now I'm scared."

She says, "You should be."

I wish they would leave each other alone.

He says to me, "You know, I heard Greenview's premiere coach was coming here to scout. I heard he is looking to fill some unexpected gaps."

Whether the coach is really coming or this is Mac's way of making himself feel important, I know for a fact he's not going anywhere. Who would drive him to practice? Greenview Premiere has never been a winning squad. But friends are friends. Sometimes I need Mac to pump me up. Sometimes he needs me. I kiss the card on the back and the front. "Well, that's too bad, because you're our star and no one is going to take you away from us. Right?"

Mac smiles. He gets up and jogs in place. "Right."

I kiss the card one more time. If I could get away with it, I would get on my knees and pray. I don't want to talk about scouts or leagues or Parker Llewellyn. I want to focus. List the presidents. Maybe do a few push-ups.

Too bad there isn't time. Coach blows his whistle and waves everyone to the far end of the field. Mac says, "Come on. Put that thing away. It doesn't play the game. We do."

Easy for him to say.

I look at Wayne one more time, wrap the card in Sam's letter, put it away, zip up the backpack, and run toward the rest of the team.

I'm nervous. Really nervous. We have imagined this moment for a long time.

We huddle around Coach. "People, people, people. We have had a phenomenal week. All of you have worked hard." He reminds the offense to look for breakaway opportunities and open men downfield. "Weave off the ball. Don't lose your cool if they get hot." They nod, and he turns to the D. "I know you're going to take care of business. They may have a star, but the rest of their offense is slow. Read the speed. Anticipate passes. If he gets close, Biggs, stick to him like glue."

Mac talks next. "As your captain, I just want you to know that you can count on me. And that there will be no big mistakes today." He looks at me and nods. "As somebody once told me, fight for what is important to you."

He holds out his hand, and we stack ours one on top of the other. We shout, "Somerset Valley rules," and then we clap our hands and take the field.

The sun is high in the sky.

No shadows.

No chance of rain.

Mischelotti sits at the end of the bench. He raises his crutch. "Good luck, Fish. I hope you don't need it."

I retie my shoes and stretch my hamstrings one more time. For the first half, we're defending my favorite goal, Wayne's net, and Greenview doesn't know that there is a dead spot right in front. If the ball hits the bald patch near the right, it won't skip to the left, no matter how much spin they put on the ball.

Greenview's center wears number 19. Historically speaking, this is not a great number. It may be prime, but James Buchanan, our nineteenth president, is generally ranked in the bottom ten.

I can beat him.

I hope.

Someone whistles. "Let's see what you got." My dad. He's standing under the tree with my mom. Next to them, Mr. Llewellyn paces back and forth, talking on his phone. From here, it looks like he's not happy with the person on the other end of that call.

Parker doesn't look all that happy either. She sits on the end of the bench, as far away from her father as possible, surrounded by her friends. Behind her and off to the side, I see a tall guy with huge shoulders and short brown hair, a Red Sox cap, and aviator sunglasses. He's wearing a Will's Delivery shirt. I try to get Mac's attention. It looks like Beer Man, but it can't be him. He has no reason to show up at our select soccer game.

The ref shouts, "Let's have a fair game." He puts the ball on the ground, blows a whistle, and my first game begins.

After two midfield changes of possession, Greenview takes control first.

Right away, it is clear that Coach was right—nineteen is the core of the team. He finds a lane and sends a perfect pass past midfield, but it's just like Coach said—their wing is slow, slow, slow—and Eddie has him covered, no sweat. The sluggish wing tries to chip one back out of trouble, but he can't escape our Mr. Biggs. His kick goes off the side of his foot, lame. Eddie charges left, dribbles around him, and with absolute precision, places the ball in front of Soup, who is running toward midfield.

"Nice work," I yell to Eddie. "Way to cover."

Soup immediately gets the ball to Mac, who does not hesitate at all. He weaves past their first line of defenders, straight toward the goal, practically unchallenged. For some reason, they're giving Mac a lot of breathing room.

I jump up and down and shuffle side to side. It doesn't matter that the ball is far away. I have to stay strong. Loose. It's never too early to check in with the D. I say to my defense, "Don't get pushed too far. Keep your eye on nineteen. If you need to kick it back to me, that's cool. As much as you can, stay between me and the ball."

It's just a precaution. Without making a single pass, Mac sets up to shoot. Their keeper dives far right—a bad move. Mac MacDonald is the king of the wide-open net.

"Goal!"

"Valley!"

"Killer time!" That's what Coach calls the first five

minutes of the game. It is the best time to drop one in the onion bag.

I love playing with Mac MacDonald.

When the game resumes, he picks up where he left off. He steals the ball and dribbles downfield with Soup to back him up. Coach goes crazy. "Give and go. Give and go," he shouts at least seven times until Mac gets trapped and passes the ball to Soup, who dribbles fast and forward, until the biggest defender steps in front of him.

Bang! Soup goes down hard, flat on his face. When he gets up, he's got his hands to his nose, and Parker runs onto the field with a white box.

He's bleeding.

Stopping play means an automatic time-out. A chance to chug some water and confer with Eddie. Soup packs his bloody nose. Coach screams "Cheap shot" at the refs.

He turns to the bench. "Parker, you're in." When she runs into position, her friends go wild.

Girls are so strange. They wave their arms and do gymnastics on the sidelines. They are all wearing shorts under skirts, which from here, look a lot like underwear. Mac says, "Greenview is going to be all over her. I just hope she can handle the pressure."

She can't. A midfielder challenges Parker one-on-one, and he trips her up. She screams foul, but it's a legal steal and she knows it. Later, she's in position, and again she is mugged. It is totally her fault. She should not be trying a left-footed crossover—which is a pretty fancy move—in that much traffic. She doesn't drag the ball far enough. Nineteen takes the ball away from her—no problem—and she hits the ground hard. He leaves her in the dust and charges up the field. Directly at me.

He is a very fast dribbler.

He has no problem with his crossover.

Obama, Bush, Clinton, Bush, Reagan. I yell "Look left," and "Close down the lane," as he gets off an early shot. The ball hits my chest and bounces at my feet. A little soft. I grab it. Easy save. No problem.

It's a little disappointing.

Not the save—but for all the hype, I was expecting something more. Three more shots—three more stops. A few people chant my name, but I wish they'd stop acting like I'm doing something extraordinary. Greenview is slow. Their star player is a dud. He hits a couple more bloopers my way. I throw the ball to Eddie, who kicks it to Parker. She can't get rid of the ball fast enough. She passes the ball to Old, who sends it straight to Mac for another score. I touch the overhead post ten times.

They should ask Mischelotti—this match has been a cakewalk.

At the half, we are winning two to zero.

Coach slaps my back, grabs me, and lifts me off the ground. In the huddle, he acts like I am the greatest thing since Election Day or free cones at Ben & Jerry's. "Ari Fish, you are hotter than a fire in the hills of Arizona." It's a weird analogy, but I don't care.

Hands hit my back, my head, my shoulders, my stomach.

Mac says, "Good job, Ari. Way to hold the lead."

I congratulate him too. "I can't believe how slow they are. I thought they'd be better. It's like the ball just rolls to my feet."

He turns away and stretches his hamstrings.

Mac never stretches. I ask, "Is something wrong?"

"I don't know. I think they're fast. Nineteen has awesome footwork, and with *her* in the lineup, he can basically shadow me. Weren't you watching? He made me trip at least three times. And I missed two open shots." When he's done publicly complaining, he whispers, "Don't tell anyone, but my legs feel slow." He looks really worried.

"I thought you handled them great." Mac never feels tired. His legs always feel fast. But I know what it's like not to feel sure of yourself. "I bet that premiere coach was just wishing he could talk you into jumping leagues."

Mac squats low and jumps up—three times. It's another drill he never does. "Yeah. He wishes."

Coach comes over and rubs my head, then wipes his hand on his pants, because my hair is a sweat sponge. "You know, if you can play like that every week, it will take a lot of pressure off your buddy right here." Then he holds up his hand and slaps me five.

Mac holds up his hand. For his turn.

Coach usually heaps on the praise, but today he has nothing to say to Mac. He walks away to talk to Parker. He slaps her five. And pats her on the back.

I know what that feels like. "Hey—did you see who else is here?" When he looks irritated, I can't believe I almost forgot. "Beer Man." I scan the sidelines, but he's gone. "At least, he was here."

"You're seeing things," Mac says. He gets up and starts walking, head down.

I jog two steps behind. "No, it was him. I swear! He was wearing the shirt. And the glasses." When Mac does not react, I know he is really upset. I say, "He was watching you." Which is not 100 percent a lie.

Mac stops. He turns around. "Why would he do that?" He scowls.

"Because you are the best man on the field. Because he knows you are a fan of his, and he is a fan of yours."

Mac rolls his eyes, but he doesn't look quite as morose as he did before. "A lot of people have that shirt."

"But who else wears that shirt and aviator sunglasses? Do they all sneak away in the middle of the game, before anyone can talk to them or ask them why they are here?"

Mac shakes his head. "The only people who come have kids on the team. Or they are friends with Coach. We would know if he had a kid—if he even knew someone on our team. And we know all of Coach's friends."

He has a valid point. "But I know it was him."

Mac does not believe in mysteries. "Come on, Ari.

Beer Man doesn't care about soccer. He doesn't care about me."

"You said you've seen him a lot. Maybe . . ."

"Maybe I'm just joking around. Ari, I appreciate what you're trying to do, but it isn't working. I am not playing well—if you don't believe me, ask Coach. Beer Man doesn't know us. It's not like we've ever seen him do anything, well, except, deliver beer."

Mac is wrong. I know it was him. "Actually, we only see him driving the truck." He may want to keep sulking, but I am not going to let him spoil my mood. "Who knows? Maybe he's the kingpin of the mob. Or the mastermind who will take over the world."

"Or maybe," Mac says, stretching one more time, "he'll be the next President of the United States."

For the rest of the game, Mac only scores once. Maybe he does lack that extra little bit of Mac-magic that everyone practically takes for granted, but it's only the first game. He is still Mac MacDonald—the best man on the field . . . by far. He has nothing to worry about, and neither do we. The truth about soccer is: Once you have a three-goal lead, no one plays that hard. No one has to.

Before we leave, Coach says, "A win like that is really nice. We have a wealth of great players. But we can't take anything for granted." He smiles at all of us. "Next week, we play East Livermore, and I want to try something fancy. So have a good weekend. Get your homework done and stay out of trouble. See you here, ready to work, on Tuesday."

Everyone claps their hands. Yes, we have a lot to do. More games to play. I don't know about fancy, but this was fun. As I pack up my gear, I smile at the sign at the end of the field. It says it all. This is the home of Wayne Timcoe. We have luck. Big luck. That's not going to be a secret for long.

ELEVEN

"Leadership to me means duty, honor, country. It means character, and it means listening from time to time."

—George H. W. Bush

On Monday, after school, Mac, Soup, Eddie, and I head into town to celebrate. Soup's shiner is blue, purple, and yellow and the piece of white tape he's supposed to wear over his nose won't stick, thanks to sweat. But unlike everyone else I know, he doesn't complain.

Eddie, on the other hand, will not stop talking. "So Ari, what do you want to do? You want to go to the Double D? Celebrate your first big victory? Or do you have something else in mind?" He trails so close he gives me a flat tire.

The Downtown Diner has been the most popular after-school hangout in Somerset Valley since the days of Wayne Timcoe. I fix my sneaker. Mac asks, "Where else would we go?"

I know for a fact Eddie gets on Mac's nerves. He says Eddie always acts desperate, almost as bad as a girl, that he should take a hint from Soup and just shut up and trust that we are not going to abandon him every time he turns his back.

The way he looks at Eddie, I have to admit I'd be paranoid too.

When we get to the diner, Soup opens the front door and stands to the side. Mac and I walk in together and grab the last two empty stools at the old-fashioned counter like they are reserved for us. Eddie and Soup stand behind us and wait for this old couple with totally empty plates to pay their bill. We spin circles and crack jokes until the kitchen door flies open and Big Dave Whittaker walks out to take our order.

Big Dave Whittaker is not called Big for nothing.

He is beyond big—the tallest, widest, shiniest man we know. He has huge biceps, and a long, thick orange-brown beard. He is the only customer in the history of my father's restaurant to finish the infamous forty-two-ounce sirloin, burp, then ask for dessert. Today he wears a white skull cap and an apron the size of a tablecloth.

He is Somerset Valley's William Howard Taft.

He is also Mac's mom's new boyfriend. According to my mother, he is the latest in a long string of "undesirable and unfortunate lapses in judgment—I can't imagine what she is thinking." Last May, when Big Dave moved in with Mac, my parents fought about it all the time.

"He has a reputation," my mom said. "Julie Biggs says he has a collection of guns. Maybe we should invite Mac to stay with us again. I definitely don't think Ari should go over there ever again."

But when I promised her that the only collections I'd heard about were trophies for weight-lifting and hot dog eating contests, and that Big Dave was turning out to be better than the last guy, that he was taking Mac fishing every Sunday morning, she stopped worrying.

Really, it was not a big deal. Mac always comes to our house. Big Dave Whittaker totally intimidates me. I stare at my menu, hoping he will not recognize me.

Mac is extremely happy to see him. "Hey Dave! What's up? Since when did you start working here?"

"Since the other day." Big Dave spills some water on the counter, and Mac quickly mops it up with his napkin. "Aren't you supposed to be in school or something?" He leans over the counter, so we can all see up close the five nautical stars tattooed on his chest. Even his neck muscles are huge. He must look pretty funny sitting on the edge of a dock with a fishing pole. But I wouldn't tell him that.

Mac drinks his water. "School ends at three."

"So does your mother know you're here? Spending her money?"

For a second, Mac's face goes blank. He says, "Yeah, she knows," but he no longer sounds happy. The truth is: Mac's mom probably doesn't know—she probably couldn't care less.

I reach into my pocket. "It's my treat."

Soup and Eddie each give Big Dave a five-dollar bill.

I hand over a ten. Mac says, "Four chocolate shakes and four crullers, please." Then he adds, "We're celebrating our first win."

Big Dave stuffs the money into his apron. He leans over the counter again, and grabs Mac behind the neck like he wants to say something important, but then he pats Mac's face, laughs, and turns away to get the crullers, the specialty of the Double D.

Mac eats his in three quick bites. "So, you think Coach is going to come up with any new plays for East Livermore? You know he hates losing to their coach."

Before I can turn my placemat into an airplane, Soup grabs it and starts drawing our favorite offenses and defenses. Last year, East Livermore beat us, three goals to two.

Eddie says, "This weekend, they trounced Mooretown," but that isn't much of an endorsement. Mooretown is a football school. Their Division One team is always fighting off league challenges by Division Two squads.

Big Dave brings the shakes, and each of us says, "Thank you very much." In the corner of the diner, Parker and her friends drink tall pink smoothies. At the same time I see her, she sees me. We both wave.

Mac sees her too. He waves too, in a fake, too-happy way. "I wouldn't be so worried about the Liver Spots, if it weren't for our little genderfication issue."

Brain freeze. I put my glass down on the counter.

Mac slurps all the way to the bottom—no problem.

"Did you see the way she messed up that pass at the end of the half? And she talks constantly—did you hear her? The whole time, she was pumping herself up. It must have driven the defenders crazy."

Eddie says, "Parker Llewellyn should have stuck with the girls' team."

"It is so unfair," Mac says. "Why do I have to be the only striker in New England to have to play with a girl?"

Through the noise, I hear Parker's voice rise and fall. I hope she is not telling her friends how nice we are. "Well, there's nothing we can do about it now."

Mac squeezes my neck the way Big Dave squeezed his. He tells everyone, "You know, the other day at lunch, she actually told Ari she was going to fight to take his place. She wanted to ask Coach for more net time."

"Is that true?" Eddie asks.

It isn't exactly true, but Eddie has milkshake all over his lip, and it is really hard to take someone seriously when they have a chocolate mustache.

I hand Eddie a napkin. Mac says, "It's her dream."

Eddie laughs.

"Exactly." Mac pulls us into a huddle. "Which just proves she's not a team player." Both Eddie and Soup agree. "Letting her play on the edges is bad enough. But if it looks like Coach is going to put her in the net, we may have to mount a protest."

I don't believe this. Protests always backfire. It doesn't matter how good your intentions are—when you organize against another kid, you get in trouble. Mac knows that.

"What are you saying?" I ask him. "That you are willing to forfeit a game?"

Soup looks like he is about to agree with me, when Mac slams his fist on the counter, and everybody jumps. "No. But you said yourself—she wants to start. And if Coach keeps putting her in, it will be a disaster." He talks really slowly, through his teeth, like he is very mad. "I need some security if I'm going to stay with this team. You understand that, don't you?"

Eddie immediately starts begging him not to jump to conclusions or do anything rash. "Whatever you want— you're our captain. Whatever you want us to do—just say the word. We need you, Mac. You have to stay with us."

This is usually enough for Mac, but today he stares at the ceiling, like there is something important up there. So we all look up too. The only thing I see is a large circular stain on one of the ceiling tiles. Mac says, "Okay. If you're game, I've got a plan."

He pulls us in a tight circle and speaks very, very softly. "Tell everyone: If she goes in the net, I'll give everyone a sign." He makes an *L* with his fingers. "We'll call it Plan Freeze-out. We won't play hard until Coach takes her out."

This is a bad idea. The worst I've ever heard. If they throw the game, we will be finished. There will be no team. But since Mac thinks it will be great, everyone agrees.

"That'll teach her," Eddie says. Too loud.

Soup tells Eddie to pipe down. "She is right over there."

Mac tells him not to worry. The diner is loud. And Coach would never consider benching them. "I'll tell the rest of the guys." Then he acts like the whole plan is going to be fun. "She won't know what hit her. I almost want you to take a game off."

Now I know he's not serious. We all care too much about the game to intentionally mess up. Mac just needs to see that his friends are on his side. He likes to act like he would take a stand, but he would never do it. The truth is, everyone can be replaced. Even him.

Big Dave takes our plates away. He asks, "You want change?"

It costs three dollars and twenty-five cents each. We all shake our heads no. I punch Mac in the arm. To show him I know this is a joke. "I play one good game, and you guys already have me replaced."

Mac twirls on his stool. "It's just hypothetical. I'm sure you're going to be great all year." He smiles. "Especially now that you have a secret lucky talisman."

"A secret what?" Eddie says loud enough for everyone to hear.

I step on Mac's foot, but either his feet are numb or he has forgotten our agreement. He better come up with something good.

"What do you mean? What's a talisman? Are you on the 'roids?" Eddie thinks he is so funny. "Haven't you heard about all those athletes who go bonkers and kill their families because they take that stuff?"

Mac says, "Biggs, you are a loon. Fish is not taking anything. A talisman is a lucky charm. Want to take a guess?" He smiles like this a game of twenty questions. No guilt. All fun. His game.

I say, "I thought you weren't going to tell."

Mac shrugs. They each take a turn.

A prize in the cereal box. A four-leaf clover. A letter from Sam.

Mac looks bored. He says, "You're all wrong. Fish got himself a Timcoe card."

In Somerset Valley, when you say the words *Timcoe* and *card,* you always attract a crowd.

Parker runs down the aisle so fast she practically knocks over a waitress. Mischelotti appears out of nowhere. Even Big Dave interrupts a customer to stand over me.

Eddie asks, "Can we see it?"

I could tell them Mac is a joker, but he would probably call me out on that.

I could say I don't have it with me.

Or I could walk out of here. This was my secret to tell—not Mac's. I could call him out and make him feel terrible. But the truth is the damage is done. I'm almost as bad as Eddie. When Mac makes me mad, I always end up apologizing. Usually before lunch.

Eddie asks again, "Well, aren't you going to show everyone?"

Mischelotti punches me in the arm. "Or are you just messing with us?"

Everyone looks at me. "I'm not messing with anyone." There's no going back now. "Give me some space."

Why shouldn't everyone know? We are a team and everyone can celebrate with me. Maybe Mac is doing me a favor.

I slowly open the front flap. I take out the plastic bag. Mac steps back, but every other eye is on my hands as I remove Sam's letter and begin to unfold it.

Slowly.

Carefully.

"Ah!" In the fluorescent light, the blue and the red glow: the lettering, *Wayne Timcoe, goalkeeper, New England,* looks 3-D.

Eddie pats my back. "Wow. I never thought I'd see one."

Soup takes a deep breath and sighs. "It's beautiful."

Mac says, "Geez, you guys, it's only a card," but then Big Dave shakes my hand so hard, my fingers tingle. "Nice going there . . . kid. I bet that's worth a couple of big bills." He wipes off the counter to a shine, and Mac steps away. I can put it down for even more people to admire.

Everyone takes a turn. When Parker finally stands next to me, we stare at the card and she breathes and says nothing at all for a very long time. "I've been searching for a Timcoe card since I started collecting. Where did you find it?"

"Ben Elliot's. Green wrapping."

She touches it with proper reverence, with her palm open. "The card shop? The one with all the cute stuffed animals in the window? I didn't know they stocked trading cards."

I tell her the entire story, the good horoscope, and Mrs. Elliot's gift. "I also have the entire 2006 Los Angeles Galaxy inaugural squad, plus a Pavel Nedved, a Franz Beckenbauer, and a Little Bird Garrincha."

"That's great."

"I know." I've never seen Parker Llewellyn this speechless.

Before she gives it back, she kisses it just the way I do, on each corner. "Thank you, Ari. You are so lucky."

My friends go berserk. "Ari's got a girlfriend, Ari's got a girlfriend." Mac looks like he wants to explode. He tells me to put it away already and that we need to get out of here. On the way home, he says, "I can't believe you let *her* touch *our* Wayne Timcoe card. I can't believe you let her kiss it."

We walk the rest of the way without saying much. I know I should give him a hard time for spilling the beans, but I have to admit, it was fun showing off Wayne.

Actually, it was great. I liked the way everyone looked at me.

I was worried for nothing. With Wayne Timcoe, my luck has only one direction: up, up, up, up, up.

TWELVE

"We grow great by dreams. All big men are dreamers."
—Woodrow Wilson

When I get home, my parents are sitting at the kitchen table. I throw my bag on the floor and go straight to the refrigerator.

Good luck makes me thirsty. "What's up?" I ask, after chugging about sixteen ounces of milk from the carton.

Mom hands me a napkin. "Sam is going to call any minute. Did you forget?"

I forgot.

I can't believe I forgot.

On the table, Mom's set up a picture of Sam with his unit. In the photo, they flex their muscles in front of a small propeller plane. Sam loves this picture. It was taken just after his first official jumping mission.

My mother stares at the phone. My father chops vegetables. In California, it is the middle of the afternoon.

When it finally rings, we all jump. Mom presses the speaker phone. "Hey Sammy. Is that you?"

He says, "Hi Mom," and he is jacked up with news.

Since his last call, he has jumped into four brush fires. All are officially contained. He has never jumped so many times in so few days, and sometimes it seems that the entire state is burning.

Then he starts coughing, and my mother is sure he's suffering from carbon monoxide inhalation. "Is there a doctor on the base? Do they check the equipment before you jump?"

His voice turns flat. "Of course there is, Mom. Of course they do. We're professionals," he says. "So, how's everything at the restaurant?" He always changes the subject when Mom questions his job.

Dad says, "We're doing a special on lamb. For all the other livestock, everything here is hunky-dory. Nothing unusual. Are they giving you enough to eat?"

We stare at the speaker phone for five silent seconds. "Yes." The tone in his voice makes it clear that we shouldn't ask about his diet either.

So Dad asks if the weather forecasts look good.

Weather is always a safe topic. Even safer than sports.

Sam tells us it's the worst fire season in years, and with the National Guard abroad, there aren't a lot of fresh recruits. They're hoping for some help from a for-hire unit from Pennsylvania or Delaware, but not to worry, everyone is smart. Last night, he slept outside and counted two hundred stars before falling asleep. He's got a blister on his foot that won't heal and sometimes his migraines act up, but otherwise, he's fine.

I think, don't tell him what to do about the blister. And don't suggest that a migraine could be something worse, like a brain tumor or a stroke waiting to happen. And above all else, don't ask the question Sam refuses to answer.

But that's exactly what my mother does. She asks it like it just popped into her head. "So, honey, have you considered coming home in time for next semester to begin?"

Sometimes when she says this, he hangs up. "Mom," he says, "I have told you a hundred times I am not coming home. I am not going back to U Mass. There is too much to do."

"Are you sure?"

"I'm sure."

"They're holding your spot."

"That's only because you insist on telling them I might change my mind."

When Sam's mad, he speaks quietly. When Dad's mad, he goes to the stove. When Mom's mad, she wrings her hands. And hands me the phone. "Ari, it's your turn to talk to your brother."

I turn off the speaker phone and hold the receiver to my ear. Sam must think I'm Dad. "She is so closed minded. After all this time, why does she still think that the only way to be a success is to—"

"Hey Sam."

"Oh. Hey buddy."

"I wish you were here. You didn't answer my e-mail. You know Mom is really proud of you. She brags about you all the time." I run up the stairs and slam the door. "I have so much to tell you!"

He coughs again. Then sighs. "So what's going on? How's the team?"

I replay every moment of the game, saving the best part for last. "But that's not the only reason I e-mailed you. Are you sitting down?"

"I am."

"I found a Timcoe."

He goes crazy. "You're joking!"

"No, it's true." I describe the card, even though he knows exactly what it looks like. "I take it to school and every game inside one of your letters. So it will give you luck too." Then I add, "Not that you need it."

Sam thinks that's funny. "Thanks, buddy. You're wrong. It is just what I need."

We talk a few more minutes, mostly about the presidents, and soccer, and Coach, and Mom's annoying habits. He says, "I'm really happy for you. And I can't wait to get my hands on that Timcoe. Can you put Mom and Dad on speaker? I really have to go."

I go back downstairs so everyone can gather around the phone. He says, "It looks like I'll be working nonstop for the next few days, so it's hard to say right now, but I'll be in touch."

Dad says, "Keep us in the loop, son."

Mom bites her nails.

Sam coughs again. "Don't worry, Mom. I'll call you soon. When I can. I know that sounds vague, but right now, it's all I can promise. Have a great game, little buddy. Trust your gut. I'll stop some fires for you. You stop some balls for me!"

He hangs up.

My mother rubs her hands together, like she wants to start a fire. "I hate to think about what might happen," she says.

My father pulls a slab of meat out of the oven and begins to carve, although even I know you're supposed to wait ten minutes. "Marjorie, our boy is doing good work. He is a smart man. He's strong. We have to believe he is going to be fine."

Friday night, I can't sleep.

I lie on my side, curled up like a ball, and stare at my alarm clock.

It is 11:08.

09.

10.

The hall light is on and my door is not totally closed. As my eyes adjust, the light seems to get brighter. And brighter. And brighter.

So I get up. Go to the bathroom. Try to pee when I really don't have to. Then I worry that if I fall asleep, I will really have to get up to pee.

I can't wait to face East Livermore.

But I can't relax. This week has been beyond fantastic.

At 11:42, I close my eyes and count to fifty. Ten minutes later, I turn on some soft music and try again. At 12:11, I curse the digital age, the digital clocks, their preciseness, their bright numbers. Why is it called a SLEEP button, if it is there to keep me awake? Somewhere I read that lying in bed with your eyes closed is seventy-five percent as good as actually sleeping. Or was it twenty-five percent?

Or am I making the whole thing up?

I turn on my reading light and study my Torah portion, until I know three entire lines by heart.

I get out of bed. Count presidents. Do fifty push-ups.

I crawl back into bed, determined to relax. I hold the blanket over my head and breathe the warm air. Sam could never sleep before a big game either. He told me that when he felt restless, he made up conscious dreams—in other words, he'd tell himself stories—with extremely good endings. I close my eyes. Maybe that will work for me.

First, Sam flies out of the sky and lands in a patch of brush near a small fire. A house sits just beyond the flames. Sam gets it under control, but then—surprise. A tree bursts into flames. The fire spreads. Sam has to step right in front of it. It is hot, so hot, but eventually, he finds a way to put it out. He walks into one house. There are two kids and their pet iguana, whose name is Jimmy, and Sam takes the pet and gives them a ride to the area school, where their anxious parents are waiting. No one dies or loses or guesses wrong.

Next, the president calls my parents to congratulate them for having one brave son. I stand on the bima at the Temple and I forget every ounce of Hebrew.

And I think I am not naked.

Then the bima becomes a net. Someone kicks a ball toward the left-hand corner.

Balls keep coming. I keep catching. I start throwing. I speak in three different languages. Mac enters a pie-eating contest. He eats seven cream pies in five minutes while Eddie Biggs sings the national anthem. Parker sits on the sidewalk. She asks, "Do you want to hang out with me? I want to hang out with you. You are the most fantastic goalkeeper in the United States of America or at least New England. And here are some chips for your sandwich."

She shakes me by the shoulder. Hard.

"Good morning, champ." Somehow, it is morning, and my father is rubbing my back, trying to wake me up. "Did you have a good night's sleep?" He opens my blinds and light invades. This morning, the sky is orange and pink and yellow. It makes thick stripes across the poster of Wayne. "Come on down and eat your cereal. Read the paper. You have a big day today. East Livermore is always tough."

My horoscope says: "This is a time for withdrawing

your energy, attention, and efforts from the outside world and external goals in order to replenish yourself. Quiet reflection and attention to your inner world, your family, and the foundation that supports all of your outside activities, is called for. This is a time to 'lie low.'"

Before Wayne, that kind of horoscope would have freaked me out. It would have made me paranoid. But now, with the power of Wayne, it doesn't.

Today is not going to be a day to lie low. It's a big day. A great day. Steve the Sports Guy tells Timid in Texas to man up and visit his granddaughter, whom he hasn't seen in three years. He tells him it takes a real man to own up to his mistakes.

In the world of advice columns, it doesn't matter if you're a guy or a girl. Family is essential; honesty is always the best policy.

I eat my cereal. If it's a little stale or soggy, I don't care. Today we play East Livermore. Wayne is in my backpack. Ten more fires are officially contained.

Nothing is going to go wrong.

~~THIRTEEN~~
FOURTEEN*

"A pound of pluck is worth a ton of luck."

—James Garfield

SOMERSET VALLEY vs. EAST LIVERMORE

AT SOMERSET VALLEY COMMUNITY FIELD
10 A.M.

The field is empty, but we are not the first to arrive. Three folding chairs sit open under the elm tree. There are new posters up and down the trunk.

Mine is on the top. *Go Ari Fish! Wipe out East Livermore!* Mac walks right past the posters without stopping.

It's not as colorful as last week's shark, but I like the way they wrote *Fish* and *Wipe out* in dark blue jagged letters.

* No unlucky Chapter Thirteen here!

I drag my stuff to the net, touch the post ten times, and begin counting presidents. Mac sits down under the tree and stretches his legs for one second each. Then he eats his breakfast. Soon there is a steady stream of cars. Eddie and Soup run full speed from the lot to the net. "Did we miss the presidents?" they ask.

Soup and Eddie have their own rituals, but now that they know about Wayne, they want to do mine too. I know for a fact Soup has at least one, but part of his ritual, of course, is not telling anyone about it. Eddie wears blue and yellow ankle tape all the way up to his knees. He tapes for every game because the one and only time he scored a goal, he was playing with a sore foot, and it was taped. It doesn't matter that there is nothing wrong with them.

One by one, everyone on the team arrives. Old joins us at Lincoln. At Harrison Two, Parker comes over and I lose my train of thought. She has dark circles under her eyes. Like she was up all night too.

We go back to George Washington. At Jimmy Carter, Coach walks toward us with his clipboard. "What's with the presidents, Fish?"

I've been counting presidents for two seasons, and Coach has never once asked me why.

"They're my inspiration. Even when I don't agree with their policies or positions, I look up to them. I know every single one in order, and I know all the important and controversial things they did. So before every game, I list them. For luck."

"I've seen a lot of odd rituals in my day, but this one takes the cake." Coach scratches his head. "But if that's what works for you, be my guest."

Eddie says, "He also has a Wayne Timcoe card. A real one. It is totally cool."

Coach grabs me by the shoulders. "Really?"

"Really." I run to the bench to grab the card. When Coach sees it, he has to hold on to the net. Of course, Coach is a huge fan.

"It's gorgeous." He gathers the entire team together and reads the bio out loud. "This is the kind of player we should all strive to become. A team player. Someone who sacrifices for the team."

"Would anyone like to touch it?" I ask. "For luck?"

Everyone lines up to feel the power of Wayne.

"It's perfect."

"We're unstoppable."

"Livermore doesn't stand a chance."

Everyone except Mac. He stands off to one side of the net and dribbles the ball. "I hate to break it to you, but a card is never going to change the way we play."

He loves breaking it to me, but I think it can and I tell him so. Since I got the card, my play has changed. Parker says, "I think it's lucky too." She takes one more turn and kisses the card.

Mac tries to balance a ball on the side of his head. It's an impossible trick, but most of the guys turn away from me and Parker, so they can cheer him on.

I don't mind. She walks with me to the bench to put the card away. We review everything we know about East Livermore's offense.

They're big.

They stick with short, accurate passes.

They almost always shoot left.

It would be stupid to admit it out loud, but I feel pretty confident. "Coach says last year, they had slow feet. See if you can exploit that." She double-knots her laces as I wrap the card in Sam's letter in the plastic bag and stuff it into the front flap.

I lean the backpack against the tree. She actually touches my shoulder with her hand. I back away. She says, "That was super-nice of you to let everyone see Wayne."

Girls are so corny. "I didn't do it to be nice. I did it for the team. I want everyone to play well." Mac jogs over and tells me to hurry—that Coach has a few more things to say. I tell Parker, "Just don't make a big deal about it. Okay?"

She starts running toward the rest of the team. "Okay."

We get to midfield just in time. "Men. Parker. This is a big one. A ferocious one. You cannot let your guards down for one minute, no. . . . one second." As he talks, Mac keeps waving me over to stand next to him. But I can't. Coach hates distractions. If I move, he'll call me out. Make me give him ten.

I stay where I am. Coach keeps talking. He reminds

us about everything he has told us in the past week. When he tells Parker that he'll put her in first chance he gets, she squeezes my shoulder. Mac looks at me like I'm Benedict Arnold.

Loud car horns interrupt the end of Coach's speech. The East Livermore cheerleaders. He spits. "Don't look. Don't listen. They are just here to intimidate you."

We all look.

It is impossible not to. There are at least eight girls. And they are all wearing short, matching skirts. At the same time, ten crows fly overhead to the Exxon sign behind me.

Coach says, "If you let them, they'll psych you out. Remember: This is our field. Your parents and friends are here. And I'll be frank. I want this one bad. I can't stand those Liver Spots. Their coach is arrogant. Wallop them every chance you get. Just keep it legal. Understand?"

Understood.

We shout, "Valley rules!" and take the field. Eddie gathers the entire back line to the net. "Have you noticed that there are suddenly a tremendous number of crows in Somerset Valley?"

No one else has noticed. I don't want to talk about the crows.

Eddie points to a wire, where a bunch of them sit. "My father says that they're here because of the environment and climate change, but to me, they're just a pain. If you hear what I'm saying."

I don't hear what he's saying. Black crows mean death. They are the symbol of bad luck. I wish he would stop talking about crows and focus on East Livermore. Their forwards are enormous.

"Watch the guy with the bright yellow hair," Mischelotti reminds the defense. "He has a reputation for playing dirty." He waves his crutch at a tall guy with hair as black as the crows'. "And that's the famous Linus Robinson." All this week, Mischelotti has tried to motivate us with amazing Linus stories. He's from New Zealand, and if we believe Mischelotti, he is as fast as Mac and maybe even stronger. Before he goes back to the bench, he says, "If you give him a second shot, you'll regret it."

At midfield, the refs look ready to go. Mac shakes hands with Linus and the yellow-haired kid too. I count a few presidents until the whistle blows. My heart beats faster. Mac takes control of the ball.

Here we go.

At first, the lanes look wide open. Old and Soup race forward, and from here, it looks like Soup has a nice line to the net. But then Soup passes to Mac, who holds the ball too long, and everything shuts down fast. No matter how fancy his footwork may be, he cannot advance the ball. The Livermore players surround him fast and keep him knotted up.

They struggle in the middle of the field, back and

forth, back and forth, until Mac loses his footing. He hits the dirt and the ball escapes. My defenders scramble into position.

We have got it covered. There are no holes.

But East Livermore is fast. They pass the ball left, then right, *pow,* then straight down the middle. I tell myself to be as smart as Sam and as fast as Wayne Timcoe. They are precise, but from the net, it's easy to see where the ball is going.

THUD.

I stop them. Five decent shots on goal. Then I bat away two more. I know it's just my imagination, but the net is starting to feel wider. Or maybe their angles are sharper. Or I'm slower. I jump up, grab another ball—a wobbly one—and yell, "Come on guys, let's get the ball out of here. I need some help."

Lincoln, McKinley, Roosevelt, Nixon.

Eddie is covered, so I send the ball to the other side of the field. I yell, "Linus charging from the left," and they swarm like bees, up and across. They don't stop running or passing the ball until it reaches midfield, where Mac is ready to take off, drive, and score.

Except that is not what happens. Mac, for some reason, holds the dribble too long. And his shots look limp. When Soup finally gets an open look, Mac's pass is way too late, which means Soup can't properly receive it. He kicks it too soon and too hard and instead of sneaking into the corner of the net, it nails a Livermore defender.

Lucky for us, the defender can't handle it either, and the ball ricochets out of bounds over the end line.

Goal kick! The crowd cheers. But not for Mac or Soup or the impending chance to score, which ends up arcing wide to the right. They are clapping for Parker. Coach is sending her in.

Right away, it's obvious that East Livermore has no real strategy for Parker. She calls for the ball, but she might as well ask for a million dollars. She is wide open, but Mac is determined to win this game without her.

Coach jumps up and down like he is going to have a conniption. He yells, "Pass the ball. Pass the ball. Mac-Donald. Pass. The. Ball."

Mac can't pretend he doesn't hear him. I can hear him. So can Soup, Parker, and the entire East Livermore offense, defense, coach, and bench. When Yellow Hair steals the ball, everyone can hear him.

"Cover the net," I yell to my defenders. "Don't leave me open." East Livermore is in a zone. They drive, three on two. Then four on three. Their passes are perfect. Out of desperation, Eddie takes a shoulder. He falls down, but the contact is deemed incidental and time doesn't stop.

I'm in trouble.

Yellow Hair passes to Linus, who accelerates and without hesitation, places the ball. It's a perfect shot. A scaring shot. It is the kind of shot that people will talk about for the next two weeks.

Unless I stop it. Or tip it. I just have to deflect it. I just have to get enough hand on that ball to keep it out of the hole.

Then no one will remember a thing.

I jump high. I reach out. I can feel the ball pushing back the tips of my fingers. My mother shouts, "Go Fish!" I try as hard as I can to hold on to that ball.

But

    I

       can't.

"Goal!"

FIFTEEN

"Our objectives are clear. Our forces are strong, and our cause is right."
—William Jefferson Clinton

At the half, Coach talks me off the ledge. "There was no way anyone—even Wayne Timcoe himself—could have caught that shot."

He fills my water bottle with Gatorade and gives me half his Power bar. It has that slightly gooey, almost melted texture. "I was so sure I had it. I thought I couldn't miss."

He empties some water onto my hands. "Let it go, Fish." He takes a deep breath. Slaps my back. "The great ones do."

After a tough half, Wayne Timcoe once said, "One lucky goal isn't enough to get me down." Now I wipe my hands on my shorts. "You're right. It's only one goal. I can hold them. We are going to be fine."

"That's right. We'll all be fine. That's what I mean." Then Coach shifts his attention to my team.

What happens next is not pretty. One by one, he calls them out. "How do you expect Fish to stop all those shots? What are you doing out there? You have to give him some support. What happened to passing the ball?" Just when I think he can't get any madder, he singles out Mac. "Have you forgotten you have teammates? Campbell was open at least twice in front of the net. And there were at least ten opportunities to pass to Llewellyn, and you didn't take advantage of a single one of them. Do you think she would be a better striker?"

It's the oldest motivational technique there is, and I know for a fact, it will never work on Mac.

His face turns bright red. He says he's the only one out there who has a shot.

"You're out of line, MacDonald," Coach yells.

"If I'm so out of line, go ahead. Put her in for me."

I follow him toward the bench. "Mac, I know you don't mean that. Just go back and tell Coach you want in." I feel sorry for him. This has got to hurt. Getting smacked down in front of everyone.

His jersey is covered in sweat. "No," Mac says. "Everyone is so into her." He kicks the ground. I've never seen him this mad or this low. "Let them see how good she is when I'm not on the field."

I remind him that we are a team and that he is our best player and that nobody can attack a net the way he does. "If you need some confidence, we could go over and get the—"

"Card?" He laughs. "Are you kidding me? No. No card. Do not get that stupid card. Coach can think whatever he wants, but she wasn't open. I'm out there doing it by myself. No support whatsoever. Let him see. I bet, after two minutes, he'll be begging me to hold the ball."

There's no use telling him that he is acting like a baby. Or that Coach is just frustrated because I let that goal in.

When Mac is this mad, you have to let him walk it off. Alone.

Before the next period begins, Coach tells me, "This is the time when true greatness comes through. You can fold right now, Fish. You can panic under the pressure. Or you can be a tribute to your presidents and Wayne Timcoe and your brother and do what they did—rise to the occasion. Take your place with the immortals."

Mischelotti sits on the edge of the bench. "It's one goal, Fish. Get over it."

I wish I had another minute to run over and touch the card, but Eddie wants to meet with the defense, and then Parker wants to ask about Mac. She wants to know if he's really mad. Or if he is just pretending. When Soup, David, and Parker go in, I don't see Mac on the bench, and I can't help wondering if he is finally going to make good on his threats and go premiere. "I hope he didn't walk," I tell Eddie.

Eddie is more pragmatic. "I hope we can hold them to one."

When the game resumes without Mac, there is a lot more passing—up the field and across it. It looks pretty, but passing is not scoring. Without Mac, little things go our way, but when it counts, every shot misses wide or high or it trickles toward the keeper.

After ten minutes and no score, I can't concentrate. Where is Mac?

I watch Parker pass the ball to Soup, who has some breathing room on the left side of the field. This is a good sign. He loves the left side. Especially with the sun on his back.

Parker moves up from midfield and she and David Old run parallel with Soup. It's a "gimme," a play right out of the book. Soup passes to Old, who, for one moment, has a wide-open lane. Coach shouts, "Make them pay! Make them pay!"

Old hits Soup in perfect position—on the run. When Soup kicks it, I am sure it will go in, but this must not be his day. The ball does not sneak into the corner of the net. Instead, it rolls right into the keeper's hands.

Eddie groans. Coach jumps up and down and then turns away, as if in pain. Mac is back, but Coach can't put him in.

We need to score a goal. Or they do. Or someone needs to set up for a goal kick. That's the only time we can make substitutions. League rules.

Jackson, Jefferson, Harrison, Nixon. Plenty of presidents have lost before they won. One loss is not the end of the world.

But then, the weirdest thing happens. After stopping a

short shot from Old, the keeper kicks it toward his stopper without taking a break. This is definitely not smart. The first rule of goalkeeping: If you have the ball, pause. Hold on to it. Even for a second. Check your defenders. Make sure they are looking. Make sure they know what you are about to do, because if you don't, the other team will.

Which is exactly what happens.

The stopper is looking the wrong way. The ball hits him in the back. Lucky Soup is in the perfect place to nab the ball, turn it around, and punch it forward. To the net. Into the net. Past the keeper and into the net.

"Goal!" We all cheer. No assist necessary.

No Mac necessary.

"Somerset Valley rules!"

Someone plays a siren. We run to midfield and hug Soup and David. "You did great," we say. I look for Parker, but she is near the sidelines, talking to her dad.

He sounds furious. "Stop focusing on the defender. Stay in your lane. Call for the ball." Everyone can hear.

I don't know what I would do if my dad cared that much. He never gives me pointers. Then again, he is a chef. According to him, a chef with two left feet.

As we scramble to get ready, Mac finally gets back in. He seems different. Happy. Ready to play. He tells Soup and even Parker and Eddie that he wants to try something new. Above all else, they must get him the ball at every opportunity. He punches me in the shoulder.

"Trust me," he says. "You do what you do. I'll take care of the rest. I know what adjustments I have to make. We've got this one nailed."

When the whistle blows, he takes control immediately. Instead of dribbling into traffic, he maneuvers the ball around two players and passes with dead-on accuracy.

He is confident. Cocky. The best player on the field.

Even though he doesn't score, Mac is back.

With a vengeance.

Second trip, he does the same thing, but this time, Soup is wide open. The entire town of Somerset Valley can see the opportunity for the little guy, but it looks like Mac has gone blind. The crowd chants, "Go to Soup, go to Soup!" Except Parker's dad. He yells, "Give it to the girl!"

Mac sprints forward. He ignores Soup. Does not see Parker. He steps up and without hesitation, kicks the melon around the stopper and right over the goalie's head.

"Goal!"

"Go Valley!"

On the field, everyone starts celebrating, laughing, and slapping five. They are slow to get back into position. This is always a bad move. Like the 1948 election. It's not over 'til it's over. They are not going to give up.

There is one minute left.

Livermore does not hesitate. The forwards sprint down the field and it seems they are more powerful too.

Mac is a step too late. Parker tries to intercept the ball, but she is too small. She tries to tip the ball, but doesn't make enough real contact to stop the momentum.

I keep my feet moving. Already, I know this game is going to be up to me and Eddie.

Yellow Hair steps into the lane, and the guy does not stop. He kicks Eddie, who pushes him back, which is not smart, because the ref is two feet away. And the push was to the face. Intentional. Dangerous.

Whistles blow.

Time stops.

"Direct penalty kick."

They set up with ten seconds to go.

Coach stays at midfield. Penalty kicks result in scores eighty percent of the time. He's thinking overtime.

But I'm not. I stand in the center of the net and stare Yellow Hair down. He can kick left, right, or over my head.

I look into his eyes. He flinches toward the center; his feet shift directions. It's a giveaway. When the whistle blows, he kicks, and I jump—full extension—as high as I can.

Another truth about soccer is: To beat the statistics, you have to know what the kicker is going to do.

Coach hugs me so tight and so hard he lifts me off the ground. "That was beautiful, Fish. Beyond amazing. You looked like you had wings."

Eddie grabs a couple of guys, and they hoist Mac onto their shoulders. They chant "Valley rules," again and again, like this was a playoff and not a regular season game.

But I don't want to celebrate. Not yet.

"Where are you going?" Mac yells, waving at me from the top of the heap. Even Mischelotti is celebrating. He leans on the Gatorade bottle and waves his crutch. "Fish, you are the man. This is your moment."

My moment can wait.

There are about twenty bags where I left mine, and most of them are black or navy blue, also like mine. I sort through the stinky sneaker mess, the T-shirts, and the sweats. It's not here. I get up and look around. Finally, I find it. For some reason, it's on the grass next to the Porta-Potty.

"Nice game," a soft voice says with a hint of Southern twang.

At first I don't recognize him. He is as tall as me. A man. Pretty muscular too. I can't tell how old he is, but he is definitely older than Sam.

"Thanks. I didn't know you liked soccer."

"Used to play a little." Beer Man bends down and picks up my water bottle, but the whole time, he is looking at the team. "You've got great instincts. That last save was something else. I thought for sure you were going to go for the fake."

I could swear he is staring at Mac. "His feet gave him

away." All goalkeepers know that the truth rests in the feet. "Mac's really good, isn't he?"

Beer Man half smiles. "You mean the striker? Yeah. He's very good. Nervy too. He's got great handling skills, and he maneuvers well, but when that midfielder had him marked, he should have passed the ball."

I don't disagree. "Mac likes to do it himself."

"He'd be wise to thread a few passes to his mates. Like that girl. Down the line, she was wide open."

Mac would have a heart attack. Beer Man wants him to pass to Parker.

I try to wave Mac over, but he's got a soda bottle now, and he's squirting everyone in sight. I say, "If you hold on a minute, I know he would like to talk to you about soccer too." Mac's going to be furious if he misses meeting Beer Man.

But before I get Mac's attention, Mom finds me. "Ari! There you are." She grabs me around the waist and squeezes as hard as she can. She gives Beer Man the evil eye while Dad pats me on the back. "You played a superior game," Dad says.

"I am so proud," she says as Beer Man walks away, no good-bye, no introduction to Mac. "You played like a champion."

Dad hands me a cream cheese brownie with chocolate chips. "Everyone kept talking about how confident you looked. How strong. How dependable. You remind them of your brother."

"Enough already, you'll give him a big head," Mac says. Now he shows up. He is drenched with soda.

"You played a fine game too, Jerry," my mom says.

I want to talk to him in private—tell him that Beer Man noticed him and gave him actual advice—but then Dad grabs us both by the neck. "Can I treat my two favorite players to milkshakes?"

"No thanks." Mac helps himself to a brownie. "I'm sorry, Mr. Fish, but I can't. Too much homework. But maybe next time."

This day cannot get any weirder. Mac never puts homework over a milkshake. I consider asking Parker to come, but I don't believe it—she's already back on the field—practicing. She dribbles in front of the net and kicks balls at her dad. Even though everyone else is packing up, she keeps working.

She dribbles left then right then *smack* into the left-hand corner of the wide-open net. I can't deny her footwork looks like she's getting faster. It would be good for her to practice shooting against a real defender.

I could probably help her out. I shout, "Do you want company?"

She must not hear me.

So I try again. "Do you want to work out together?"

She looks. At me. Then her dad. Shakes her head. A flock of crows flies over the Home of Wayne Timcoe sign. It needs a coat of paint. "No. I'm okay. But thanks."

I wave good-bye. Fine. Suit yourself, Parker Llewellyn. Truth is I didn't really want to stay anyway.

I want to go home.

I want to write to Sam.

I want to relish each moment of this perfect, perfect day.

SIXTEEN

"Next to the right of liberty, the right of property is the most important individual right guaranteed by the Constitution and the one which, united with that of personal liberty, has contributed more to the growth of civilization than any other institution established by the human race."

—William Howard Taft

Under the Wayne Timcoe poster, I dump my bag. Gum wrappers, sweaty socks, an old wet shirt. My water bottle leaks a last few drops of orange. I tell the poster, "I got the penalty kick. I was the best player on the field."

In the front flap: gum, two pens, my pocket guide to the presidents.

That's odd. I'd bet a million bucks that Wayne was there. In the front flap. In the plastic bag. In Sam's letter. Where I always keep him.

I open the back flap, the side pockets, the little secret zipper pocket near the top. Nothing. None of it is here. I tip my bag upside down and shake. I check every pocket.

The bag is empty.

Even though I know I brought the card with me, I look in my top drawer and pull out every single one of my cards.

I have 157, including Wayne.

Now I have 156.

Wayne Timcoe, where are you? I am about to lose it.

I review my day. I took it to the field. We passed the card around. When everyone was done, I wrapped it up and put it back. I zippered the flap. I know I did. I made sure it was safe. The Wayne Timcoe poster looks down on me.

"It has to be here." I sift through every piece of paper, every shirt, towel, and sock one more time. When you are stressed out, it's easy to miss something. Mom always says, "The third time you look in the same place, you'll find what you are looking for."

So I look three more times.

It can't be gone.

But it is.

What usually happens when my luck turns sour:

I call Mac.

He comes to my house.

He solves the problem.

We get a milkshake.

What happens today:

Big Dave answers the phone. "Can you call back later?"

Click.

Dial tone.

I sit for one minute, which, in my dictionary, is technically later. He picks up on the fourth ring. "What? Didn't I just say—"

"I'm sorry to bother you, but I would appreciate it if I could speak to Mac for just a minute." I talk very fast. "I wouldn't ask if it wasn't really, really important."

He asks, "Is your house on fire?"

"No."

"Then it isn't an emergency."

I pretend that he is someone else. Someone small. And nice. With small hands and no tattoos. I picture him sitting on the dock fishing with Mac. I tell myself his bad mood is a figment of my imagination. "If you just let me talk to him, I promise I'll make it quick."

He groans. The phone goes silent. I try not to read into it.

While I wait, I scan my room again, the top of my desk and underneath my bed, even though I know it is not in either location. Even though there is no chance my Wayne Timcoe All-Star League trading card is in my room, I go through every drawer while I wait for Mac to come to the phone.

Click.

Dial tone. When things go bad, they go really bad.

This time when I call, Mac's mom picks up on the first ring. She sounds tired. "Ari, it's been a long day. Can you talk to him tomorrow?"

It's not cool to beg, but she leaves me no choice. "I just need to talk to him for one minute. Please. It's urgent."

She yells, "It's urgent!"

There are no familiar sounds, like Mac running to the phone or his mom telling him to hurry up and take care of business, for god's sake. I prepare to apologize, for bugging him when he said he didn't want to go out, for calling when he is busy, for not letting Big Dave take his extremely important call uninterrupted, but then his mom comes back on and says, "Honestly, make it fast," in a tone that requires no guesswork.

But at least Mac picks up. "What's the matter?"

I try not to freak out. "I need you to come to the field. Now. It's an emergency. Wayne is missing."

For exactly four seconds, he says nothing.

"Are you there? Hello? Did you hear me? The card is gone. I looked everywhere. It was in my backpack and now it's not. Can you come over and look with me? I think I must have dropped it."

Seventeen seconds of total silence. Then footsteps. Soft voices. Then more steps. "I'm really sorry," he says, "but I can't."

Deep breath. "I'll talk to your mom."

"I can't do it."

"Mac, can you just ask?"

When he comes back, he doesn't sound any different. "My mom says I'm not allowed to go anywhere. She thinks I'm not meeting my potential, and I'm not going anywhere extra until my grades improve."

Mac's mom has never cared about his potential before. She usually loves when he comes to our house. "But did you tell her? That this was an emergency? I'm sure she'll—"

"No. Yes. Look, Ari, I'm sorry. Deal with it. I can't come. She doesn't care about your trading card." When I start to beg again, he sighs. "Are you sure you looked everywhere? Did you check your bag?"

"Yes. Of course I checked my bag. Three times. And every drawer in my room, even though I know we—"

"What about the car?"

No. The car! Of course! It's a good idea. "Bye," I say, and hang up the phone. I run to the car, but the floors are clean, the seats uncluttered. The card is not on the floor. It is not under the mats. It's not stuck in the seat or the glove compartment or the crack behind the cup holder. The windows are shut.

The card has to be at the field. If I go over there, I'm going to find it, and everything will be okay.

I pick up the phone to call him, but there's no point. I get the message. He is not coming with me.

I listen to the dial tone. A long flat line.

SEVENTEEN

"When you are in any contest you should work as if there were—to the very last minute—a chance to lose it."

—Dwight D. Eisenhower

I run downstairs, almost smack into Mom. She is carrying an overflowing basket of laundry. Wrinkled shirts tumble to the floor.

"Sorry." I pick up the clothes, dump them back into the basket, and talk fast. "Mom. I need to go back to the field. I lost one of my trading cards. I know I brought it to the game, and now I can't find it. I must have dropped it. It was in my bag—but now it's not."

She walks to her room, dumps the clothes on her bed, and begins folding. No sympathy. "Honey, you have so many of those cards. Do we really need to go to the field? You have schoolwork. I'm tired. And your father needs to get to the restaurant. What if I give you some money? You can buy another pack later." She notices a faded grease stain on one of Dad's shirts, balls it up, and tosses it into the corner basket.

I grab the next shirt and fold it the way she likes it—with the buttons up and the arms in the back. "Mom. Please. It's not just any card." I fold a pair of pants and find two sock matches. "It was a Wayne Timcoe."

My dad walks into the room. "Ari? Did you just say you had a Wayne Timcoe card? You're pulling my leg. Let's see it. That card is supposed to be valuable."

"What do you mean, valuable?" Mom asks. "Ari, if you found something valuable, why didn't you tell us?"

Now I feel stupid. "I didn't find it. Mrs. Elliot gave it to me. And I don't know. I just didn't. You have other things on your mind."

Dad grabs my mom and makes for the stairs. "Come on. Let's go."

She still won't believe it. "Are you sure you lost it? You never lose anything . . . you've always been so careful with your things."

Thank God, Dad drives. As we pull into the parking lot, he says, "Don't worry, Ari, if it's here, we'll find it."

An old gray car speeds away, but the field is not empty. Parker is still here, and now she's sprinting around cones. Seven balls sit in the back of the net. When she sees me, she runs to the elm tree. "What are you doing here?" she asks.

She sounds a little annoyed.

"The Timcoe card . . . it's gone."

I don't need to say anything else. We get down on our knees, and together, we comb through the grass near the tree and every bench. Under the bleachers. Near the net. My parents check out the bathrooms. We start running when my mother yells, "Ari. Come over here. I think we found something."

It's the letter from Sam, and it is wet and soiled and decomposing as we speak. My dad holds it as far away from his nose as possible. "It was where you think it was. Near the top. Crumpled up in a ball. Disgusting."

Beyond disgusting.

Dad returns to the Porta-Potty to throw it away. Mom says, "Don't worry—the card wasn't there. Your father looked." She pinches her nose, but it's not funny. "I made him stir."

I want to scream. Parker grabs my arm. "Come on. Let's check the field."

That seems too crazy, too illogical, but if I don't do something, I'm going to scream. We leave my parents to search through the garbage cans and run as fast as we can, and the crows fly away in all directions.

There is nothing on the grass. If Parker weren't here, I'd probably cry.

But she is. So I keep looking, until we both have to admit, it's pointless. The letter did not accidentally flutter into the Porta-Potty, and the card did not fall out of my backpack onto the field. I lie down and stare at the sky. Parker sits down next to me and stretches her legs. She is wearing the cleats I wanted, the latest detachable kangaroo leather cleats for advanced players. Her father is gone. I ask, "What are you still doing here anyway?"

"Practicing."

"No one likes soccer that much."

"You don't have anything to prove." When she straightens her knee, her muscles bulge. She does the same thing to the other leg, then puts her arm behind her back to stretch her triceps. "I always loved playing soccer, and playing on this team with players like you was my dream. But lately, it feels more like a nightmare." She shakes out her arms and pulls up a big clump of grass. "Even practice is frustrating. When I'm wide open, no one passes to me."

"That's just part of being new to the team—you know that."

She sighs. "My dad says they're doing it on purpose, and that I have to push the issue with Coach. I asked him if I should go back to the girls' league, but he says that now that I've committed to the team, I have to stick with it. Otherwise I'll look like a quitter." She sighs. "It's a lot of pressure."

I look at my parents, who are now sifting through garbage. They couldn't care less about soccer. They tell me all the time, "We just want you to be happy and healthy," which also means I can play soccer only as long as I have a bar mitzvah, get good grades, and go to college. Last year, when I was hoping for new cleats, I got a leather laptop case instead.

I think I see something small flicker near the opposite

net, but it's a supermarket receipt, not the card. I shout, "Wayne Timcoe, where are you?" Parker startles extremely easily, which makes me laugh. "What are you so nervous about?"

She shakes her head. "Nothing. I'm just tired, and you yelled really loud." She rolls onto her stomach and props her chin in her hands. "Tell me the truth. Are your friends ever going to stop laughing at me?"

It is nicer to lie. "They don't laugh."

"Mac does."

"Well, he's different. You just have to understand—"

"Don't try to tell me he's insecure. Or that once I pass his test, he'll be nicer. When you let me touch the card, he looked like he wanted to explode."

Girls are so sensitive! "You have to understand, he's just looking out for me. He's my oldest friend—we're practically brothers. He sticks with me; I stick with him."

She looks skeptical. "But you're so different."

I forget she's new in town, that she doesn't know everything. "Mac didn't always have it so good. His mom, if you haven't noticed, is really young."

"When would I have noticed? She's never here. My dad wanted to talk to her, but he couldn't find her. Coach told him that she doesn't come to the games. I was sure he was lying—sometimes my dad makes a scene. But then she didn't return his calls."

"She must have been working. When she's not busy, she comes to our games."

I'm lying. The truth is, Mac's mom doesn't come to anything—not even the playoffs. She doesn't drive unless my parents can't, which is basically never. And I would never tell Parker, but once she spent a night in jail.

But maybe things will change. Maybe now that she has Big Dave, she'll be able to relax. Maybe he'll be the dad Mac never had, or better yet, his real dad will finally come home. We never talk about it, but deep down inside, I know that's what he wants. His dad. Or at least, *a* dad. Someone who will stand on the side and cheer for him.

My parents finish what they are doing and go back to the van. They don't call out to us. They don't even wave. This is unofficially the longest conversation I have ever had with a girl in my entire life. Even if we are talking about Mac, we are talking.

They are the best parents in the world.

I say, "You know, he could play premiere, but he doesn't."

Parker doesn't think this is so special. "If he played premiere, he wouldn't be the star of the team."

"If he played premiere, we would probably have lost today." That gets her. "Look," I say. "Do me a favor and stop worrying about Mac. Eventually, he'll deal. You'll be friends. He has to. It's a rule."

Now she laughs. "What rule is that, Ari?"

"The team always comes first rule."

She thinks about this for a minute. "So let me get this

straight—now you want me to believe that none of you ever put yourselves above the team?"

"When you put it that way, no. Of course not. But when it's necessary, we all suck it up. So even if he thinks you should have stuck with the girls' team . . ."

"Which he does."

"Could you let me finish?" She nods. "Even if he thinks that, he won't jeopardize our record." I am absolutely one hundred percent positive this is true. Plan Freeze-out is just a joke. "He may complain. He may act like a jerk. He'll even threaten to change teams. But he won't leave. And neither should you." I can't believe I just said that. "I mean, that's the rule. But don't. Okay? You're good. Really good. You just need a little more confidence."

This is so embarrassing.

I'm the one with no confidence.

But she doesn't bring that up. "Really? Do you think so? Last week, I should have had that guy. I should have cut the ball with my heel, but I blew it."

"You just slipped up. Next time, you'll do it. You just can't let them intimidate you." I am sure she is going to bring up her dream to take my spot, but she doesn't. Today, she nods with enthusiasm.

"That is exactly what my friend told me. He said I'm overcompensating and getting intimidated."

"Your friend?"

She half smiles. "Just this guy who helps me out once in a while."

"Sounds serious."

"Not really."

I have to admit, I'm jealous. Mac never wants to take extra practice—he doesn't need it—and if he won't, Eddie and Soup would rather not either. "If you guys ever need a keeper, I'm free after practice."

She bites her lip. Then she looks away. When the silence becomes awkward, she says, "Thanks. That would be great." When I smile, she does not smile back. Instead, she looks beyond me to the double *x*. "If it works out, I'll let you know." She doesn't mean it.

Maybe her dad hired a college student to coach her. "I mean, if your dad's paying, I'm happy to pitch in and all. I'm not looking for a handout."

Now she looks totally uncomfortable, like her beautiful cleats are on fire and she wants to get out of here. I change the subject. "You know, I'm surprised the newspaper hasn't been around. You would think they'd be all over you. Front page."

Parker has an extremely nice smile. "My dad won't let them. He won't let them cover me until I'm starting." She rolls onto her back, and pushes with her hands and feet into a perfect arch. Her shirt inches up. I stand up and look away. If I don't, I'll turn purple. "He says they'll turn me into a curiosity. That I have to do more than just make the team. He wants me to score. That is, if I can't play in the net."

Her face turns red.

I'm sure mine is too. "Right now, all I can think about is finding Wayne Timcoe. Without him, your dream will come true and you will be in the net." We walk around and stare at the grass, even though we know the card is not here.

She asks, "You're not afraid, are you? That without the card, you can't play?"

I guess it's obvious. "Of course I am. If it's gone for good, I'll stink. We'll lose games. I'll go back to the bench. My friends will hate me."

She doesn't laugh.

I say, "I just don't understand it. I put that card in my backpack, I know I did. No one else touched it."

Parker stops walking. "That's not true."

"What do you mean?"

"I mean Mac had your backpack."

"No he didn't."

"Yes he did. During the break. He took your blue bag. Ari, I'm sorry, but I don't think he cares as much about the team as you think he does. I thought you knew. He took your backpack and he took it into the bathroom. I saw the whole thing."

As the sun goes down, reality sinks in.

Somebody stole my card. Somebody on my team. Somebody who knew it was lucky, who knew how important it was.

I did not drop it. I did not lose it.

The card was in the backpack, but only two people knew exactly where it was.

One was Parker. The other was Mac. He knew exactly where I put my stuff. And he has been acting strange. Only Mac thought the card was a joke. Only Mac touched my stuff.

Mac.

It is the worst feeling in the world, beyond falling off a cliff or standing in pitch-black darkness, not knowing which way to walk. It's like getting caught alone in a fire, when you were sure someone had your back.

If there is another answer, I don't see it.

Mac is a liar. His mother didn't ground him.

Mac doesn't care about the team. Or me.

Mac stole my card.

EIGHTEEN

"The new frontier of which I speak is not a set of promises—it is a set of challenges."
—John F. Kennedy

How to fake illness in order to avoid seeing your friend, whom you suspect of stealing your most important possession:

- Take a steaming hot shower. Cough until your voice sounds scratchy.
- Put a sweatshirt on. Keep the heat in. Shuffle down the stairs and look as sad and pathetic as you possibly can.
- Pray that Mom is too busy to notice.

When these techniques do not work, try honesty.

"I don't want to go to school. Please. I don't want to face Mac. I think he stole Wayne Timcoe."

My father is usually in my corner, but today he plays the skeptic. "Are you sure?" He beckons me to the stove. He is stirring oatmeal. "That doesn't sound like Mac."

I say, "He wouldn't help me look. He's been acting really weird."

"Ari, that's not evidence. Maybe he has other things on his mind."

Mom, of course, is practical. "You're going to have to face the music sometime. If you wait, it will only get worse."

I look through the paper. There are one hundred and seventy-one fires burning in California.

My horoscope makes me ill: "The New Moon in Libra helps you discern if someone is sincere. You could decide that someone new in your life is not worthy of your time. If you visit a sick relative or friend, forget the flowers. Bring a book of puzzles instead—something to keep their mind busy."

My mother sits at the table and stares at her laptop. She clicks a few keys, then slams the lid shut. "It's been an entire week. Why hasn't Sam written? Where is he? Why don't you just talk to Mac?"

Dad pours a glop of oatmeal into a bowl, and I eat it with extra sugar and milk, no raisins. He says, "Son, your mother's right. You guys just have to sit down and talk. Together, you'll figure it out. You always do."

Maybe I walk too slowly. Or maybe Mac doesn't see me coming. Maybe once the sine wave of luck turns, there is nothing anyone can do to stop the momentum.

All I know is when I get to Mac's house, he's already

walking out the door with a soccer ball. Even though it is Monday and we do not have practice. I ask, "Weren't you going to wait for me?" I sound pathetic.

He doesn't look particularly guilty. "Hey. Let's go," he says, without breaking stride or razzing me. I swear my fever spikes for real.

At the same time, Big Dave and Mac's mom walk out the front door. They look like they are dressed for the beach. They get into their car and pull up beside us.

"Can we have a ride?" Mac asks.

"Heck no," Big Dave says. "Just washed this car."

His mother looks like Jackie O with her big sunglasses and hair tied back. "Don't forget we won't be home until late. So have a good time. I left you a ten-dollar bill. So get yourself something to eat after practice. If you want, sleep over at Ari's." She winks at me. "I'm sure your parents won't mind."

Big Dave revs the engine. "If you go to the Double D, remember—they think I'm sick. Don't mess that up." They drive off.

I should feel sorry for him. "It's Monday. We don't have practice."

Mac stoops down and ties his shoes. When he gets up, he doesn't look me in the eye. "I'm going to the field anyway. I didn't know I needed your permission."

"You don't."

Mac never takes extra practice. He never cops an attitude like this with me. It takes work to keep up with him.

He asks, "So, did you find your card?"

"No."

He drops the ball, kicks it high into the air, and catches it with one hand. "Maybe now you'll see that the card wasn't really magic. No offense, but if you want a lucky charm, you should go to the field and hunt for a four-leaf clover."

He laughs. I'm offended. "I searched the car. I covered every inch of the field. The only explanation that Parker and I could come up with—"

"You called Parker?"

"No." I don't know why I'm the one acting defensive when he is the one acting guilty. "She was at the field. Running the cones. When I told her what happened, she helped." She acted like a friend. "You know, she takes extra practice every night. Maybe you should try playing with her."

The rest of the way, we do not talk. He dribbles his soccer ball and doesn't pass it to me once. I count presidents who betrayed our country, who didn't understand the importance of the truth or morality or honesty.

It is not easy walking eight blocks with the person who just stole your most valuable possession, but I do it. It's a Pisces thing. We're compromisers. We don't confront anyone unless absolutely necessary. I try to make conversation, but every topic I start ends with long, awkward silences.

When we get to school, Parker is waiting. She is wearing her limited edition vintage Wayne Timcoe T-shirt. I speed up; Mac slows down. He calls out to a couple of girls. He does not say hello to Parker.

She says, "Tell me you found it."

"Not yet." My voice cracks.

If she steps any closer, we'll be touching. "Did you talk to him?"

"No."

"You didn't even ask him?"

"No."

Now Parker puts her hands on her hips and scowls. She's clearly mad, and in a weird way, it is sort of cute. Until I turn around and see why. Mac is here. He drops his bag. "Ask who about what?"

"Ask you about Ari's Wayne Timcoe card. Did you know it was missing?"

"Yeah. I know."

This can't be happening. This is not the way I wanted this to come out.

But it's too late now. Neither one of them is going to back down. Parker asks, "And how do you think it disappeared?"

Our friends gather around. Mac says, "I don't know. Maybe someone took it. Someone who is having trouble with their crossover dribbles?"

Eddie tries not to laugh. Parker doesn't cave. "Actually, I think it was someone who couldn't stand sharing the spotlight." Eddie shakes his head. Soup stuffs his hands in his pockets. They all look at me.

The last time I felt this cornered was over a year ago. I had just lost the starting job to Mischelotti. Sam said, "You must always take a strong, confident stance." It was a hot, sticky night, and he was home for two days. "Watch the eyes and the feet. Beware of tricks. A lot can happen in a season." He kicked the ball hard, and I caught it. "When the chips are down, I know you'll make me proud."

Now the chips are beyond down. Mac looks upset. I wonder if maybe he didn't take it. If I am about to accuse my friend for a crime he did not commit.

He stands with my friends. They all face me. Except Eddie. He looks up at the sky. Maybe for crows. Mac says, "Say what you want to say, Ari."

Parker says, "Come on, Ari. Ask him."

She is not helping. "Do you have my Wayne Timcoe card?"

Mac's nostrils flare. He throws the ball at Soup, and steps forward—way too close—so we are standing eye to eye. "Do you really think I stole your card?" When I don't answer, he steps back and smiles at everyone else, grabs the ball, and twirls it on his finger. Victorious. "Seriously, does anyone really think I needed a piece of cardboard to make me a good player?"

My friends laugh. Of course they don't. Mac doesn't need luck. They don't care about his nostrils. He is a winner. The leader. The captain of our team. If anyone needed a lucky card, it was me.

It still is.

I start to panic. "Maybe it was supposed to be a joke. Or maybe you were mad. I don't need to know how, and I don't care why. But you're acting weird."

I don't know why I thought Mac would confess. He is too proud. He does not want or need any of my loopholes, even though plenty of presidents would have jumped through less.

There is no easy way out of this. It is impossible to back down completely. "Did you find it?"

He smiles. "No."

My shoulders feel heavy. This is worse than losing a game. As our team walks away, Parker does not seem upset at all. "Trust me," she says. "It's going to all work out. A person who stands for nothing will fall for anything."

"Is that supposed to make me feel better?"

She shakes her head. "I guess not. But I still think it's true. I got that off a fortune cookie."

"Great." We slowly walk to our lockers. I trip on a crack. In the halls, the lights flicker. That gives me a headache.

Parker thinks I'm looking for reasons to be depressed. I tell her, "You think I was unlucky before? Just wait. I know I'm going to regret this day."

There are a few holy rules for guys:

1. The team always comes first.

2. Don't turn your back on a guy. Don't accuse him of anything you can't prove in a court of law. Don't let a girl come between friends.
3. Never talk at the urinals. (If your friend leaves his fly down, don't say anything. Don't look. Don't do anything.)
4. Don't share an umbrella. Even if it's pouring.
5. The lunch table is sacred. You sit there if you belong. If you don't, go somewhere else. In other words: See rule one. The team always comes first.

Break one of these rules, and you are toast. Unless, of course, you are the top dog, the kingpin, the most important person in your group.

Then, face it: You can do whatever you want.

In social studies, triangle-shaped notes fly between Mac and Eddie, and Mac and Soup, but not to me. Even when my hand is up, Mr. Sigley calls on someone else. In the hall, Mac walks between Soup and Eddie to class. He jokes around with Eddie, even though normally, he would joke with me.

In math, we have a pop quiz. I know I got at least two questions wrong.

The news is everywhere. In the hall. In class. People whisper as I walk by:

Ari Fish had a Wayne Timcoe card. Mac MacDonald stole it. Parker Llewellyn walked up to Mac this morning and told him he was a thief, and Ari Fish took her side.

There is black duct tape all over my locker. I have to

peel it off, just to open the door. It leaves a sticky residue. They didn't stop there. Inside, all my books are crammed onto one shelf. Today's homework is crumpled up in a ball. My sandwich is squished. I throw it away.

I want to cry. I want to punch someone. Eddie leaves me one note: "Just tell him you didn't mean it. Before it's too late." I want to call my mother and tell her I really am sick.

The bell rings.

My luck is gone.

It's time for lunch.

NINETEEN

"An injured friend is the bitterest of foes."
—Thomas Jefferson

Parker intercepts me at the cashier. I'm counting out pennies, apologizing to everyone behind me. "I'm sorry, really sorry," I say to the lunch lady, who will not stop tapping her foot. Counting coins slows everything down. I say, "I thought I had money in my canteen."

"Well, you don't."

I am up to seven *really*'s and four *sorry*'s when Parker reaches into her pocket. "Here. I have a dollar. Does that get you off the hook?"

It gets me off the hook with the lunch lady, but I'm not sure I want Parker Llewellyn helping me quite so much. I definitely don't think we should sit together by ourselves in the cafeteria.

She obviously thinks otherwise. "Ari, I have to tell you everyone is talking about you and Mac. They can't believe he took your card. They think you totally did the right thing. Here—let's go sit at my table."

I shake my head. This is not a game, and Mac and I

have never had a serious argument. When we disagree, it's always about little stuff. If I let this drag on, it is only going to get worse.

I tell Parker, "I don't think that's a good idea." My regular table is almost full. Mac is there, and so are Soup and David and Mischelotti, who under normal circumstances, sits with the lacrosse team. "It's not that I don't appreciate the offer, but . . ."

"But what?"

"Parker, what you did this morning was gutsy, but it wasn't exactly . . ."

"What? What are you saying? Are you mad because—"

"No. I'm not mad." Girls! "But you have to trust me on this. Right now, I have to sit at my table." I thought I had already explained this. "If I don't, it would be like saying that I don't care about the team. Don't take this the wrong way, but this is about more than Wayne Timcoe. We don't want to wreck the team."

"What is that supposed to mean—don't take this the wrong way?" She stands extremely close, and everyone from my table stares. "The team is already wrecked. Your so-called team walked out on you. It fell apart when your friend stole your card." She crosses her arms across her chest and a couple of the guys laugh. "You're going to blame this on me, aren't you?"

"No, I'm not."

"Then don't let him get away with it. Sit with me."

"No. I can't."

"Yes you can."

This is ridiculous. "No, I can't." She walks away, most likely in disgust. I stand in front of my regular table. I envision a ball coming toward the net. When Mac pauses in the middle of an old story, I say, "Hey guys, how's it going?"

If everything was okay, they would say hello. Or rib me. They would make fun of Parker or my tray full of cafeteria food or the fact that I had no money.

They would tell me to shut up—Mac is telling a story.

Today, they do not say anything. Mac continues to tell his story, as if I were a fly or another household pest. My friends' faces stay glued to Mac's, and they all look interested, even though the story is an old one.

I know it.

They know it.

There is one empty seat. It is at the far end of the table, across from Eddie, and if Soup will just push his chair in one inch, I can get there without interrupting again.

All I need is one inch. "Can you give me some space?" I ask.

Eddie looks like he is about to throw up. Soup looks smaller than usual.

I want that empty seat. This time I talk louder. "Excuse me."

Soup scrunches forward, but otherwise, no one else moves. It's tight. Especially when I try to shuffle behind Mischelotti. He scoots his chair back, so I can't sit. I can't move. "So Pickled Herring, how are you doing?"

"I'm fine. Can you give me some space?" Mischelotti scoots his chair forward, so I can get by. Before I sit, I look around. It wouldn't be the first time Mac told someone to put a thumbtack or something disgusting on someone's chair. It wouldn't be the first time he sacrificed a friend to a prank.

Eddie looks at me for a split second, a sorry-it's-your-turn gaze. Unlike everyone else at the table, he knows what this feels like.

"The guy is a liability," Mac said after last year's first loss. "If it weren't for Biggs, we would have won. If he calls me one more time, I'm going to scream."

This wasn't true. It was the offense that lost us the game. Eddie was the best we had.

But I didn't say that.

Instead, when Mac told me to fill Eddie's locker with golf balls, I thought, why not? What was the harm? It was just a prank. Mac said it would help Eddie toughen up. I convinced myself that he would think it was hilarious. This is what teammates did. For fun.

Now I know how much fun it must have been.

My hot lunch smells burnt. The gravy is the consistency of glue. I swirl it into the gray potato mush and vow to make sure my sandwich is, first and foremost, unsquishable.

Eddie looks at my tray and very quietly says, "Sorry."

Mac does not acknowledge me. Instead, he launches

into the Mia-Hamm-in-the-elevator story. We have each heard this tale at least a hundred times. It's a stupid story, with three separate endings, but no one says, "That's an old one, Mac. You've told us that one before, Mac. Are you sure that really happened, Mac?"

My appetite is gone. I don't want to hear this story. I don't want to watch my friends pretend that this story is new. I definitely don't want to act like nothing's wrong.

I stand up. "See you later, guys," I say, even though Mac will not stop talking, even though no one else says good-bye.

And for a second, I think I can do it. I can walk away. I don't have to listen or watch or feel sorry for myself. I hold my tray and walk back toward the aisle and hope that Soup does not scoot his chair back.

Then the foot comes out. Or maybe it's a crutch. It doesn't really matter. Mac loves to score. If he wanted to make a fool out of me, this is the easiest shot there is.

There is no defense. You can't stop your flying tray or your knees or your hands from hitting the ground. You can't stop your food from splattering in all directions.

It's momentum.

There is only so much you can do.

I brush myself off.

I pick up the tray.

I walk away. No applause.

When Mac finishes the story, everyone laughs.

• • •

For four days straight, I walk to school alone. I don't talk to Mac. I eat lunch in the library by myself and fold planes, but they all hit the ground, nose first. In social studies, we have statewide testing. I fill in circle after circle with my number two pencil and write essays about passages I don't completely understand. It's hard to concentrate. I go to class, but I don't raise my hand.

For four days straight, I go to practice, but only Coach and Parker speak directly to me. We win a midweek game, two to nothing, but Parker says the victory feels shallow, under the circumstances. I wait for her to invite me to practice with her and her friend, but she never does.

This gives me plenty of time to learn my Hebrew. By the middle of the week, I've got the entire passage memorized.

The rabbi thinks this is absolutely fabulous. "Let's talk about your speech." In case I am not sure if my mother has told him what is going on, he says, "You know, Ari, throughout your life, you will accept many jobs. Some of them will be fun. Some won't."

He waits. I know he is waiting for me to ask a question. He's a rabbi. He tells all the students, "I live for questions."

Mine is sort of lame. "Can I be honest? I wish I were reading a story. Like Adam and Eve. Or Joseph and his coat. This whole census is sort of boring."

Of course, the rabbi is honest too. "Ari, there are no coincidences when it comes to the Torah. Trust me.

When you least expect it, you will understand why Naso is a perfect portion for you." He tells me to think about the reading and think about my own responsibilities. "You know, in the Torah, God gives responsibilities to the people who can handle them."

"Just don't call them blessings in disguise," I say. When he laughs, I figure that was exactly what he was going to say. "Because they seem more like burdens to me."

"Burdens?" The rabbi acts like I just said the magic word. "What about burdens, Ari? Do you think the Hebrews thought carrying the Tabernacle was a burden? What does it feel like when someone gives you a responsibility that is too big? Can you relate that to something like that in your own life? Maybe soccer? Your mom says that you and your friend—"

"Soccer's not a burden." I love playing keeper. Even if my friends never speak to me again, I require no convincing. I can play on a team of rivals.

"Just think about it," the rabbi says. "You certainly have been given some special responsibilities on the field—and off. Are they blessings? Or burdens? What about your brother? Is what he does both a blessing and a burden too?"

My mother needs to tell him a whole lot less. This is way more personal than I want to get. Sam chose his job. I'm dealing with the team. But when it comes to talking to the rabbi, it's best to be polite. "Thanks, Rabbi," I say, "I will think about it."

He tries to look parental. "Good. You know, sometimes, Ari, what you think is a burden can become an opportunity." This is rabbi-speak for "chin up."

That may be true for the Torah, but after four straight days, there are no new opportunities waiting for me. Nothing has changed. Eddie is the only one brave enough to say anything to me, and the only thing he says is "Hi," or "Good game," and that's only if no one is around. He doesn't dare save me a seat. Or walk with me in the hall. Or even signal to me during practice, which means we are too sloppy for Coach. Mischelotti gives Mac a ride to school and the field. This week, I have e-mailed Sam seventeen times. "Help! I need to talk to you!" But he does not call.

On the way to the field, Parker asks what I'm going to do next, if I have a plan, a strategy, a line of attack that will blow Mac MacDonald out of the water. I say, "Parker. Stop. I don't know. How am I supposed to prove that he has it?"

And that makes *her* mad.

I wonder what I would do if I could go back in time, before Ben Elliot's, the green pack of cards, the good horoscope. If I knew then what I know now, what would I do? Would I still want that card? What if I had never held that card?

If that isn't a burden, it's a very good question.

TWENTY

Saturday morning, there is finally an e-mail from Sam.

> No time to write or call.
> But I am fine.
> Just got another call, so I'm off to another fire.
> Look up into the sky and pretend you see me.
> Fight to the end for what is important to you.
> Sam

"Scroll down, Dad, there are pictures too." In one, the smokejumpers stand shoulder to shoulder. In another, they sit in a helicopter, suited up, ready to go.

Sam is third from the right. His shoulders are back. His smile is so big his eyes are closed. His hair is short.

I ask, "When did he do that?"

Dad stares at the pictures and says, "I don't know."

He walks to the counter. There is a bag full of apples in the sink. He starts coring. It has been almost two weeks since Sam called, even longer since he wrote a real letter.

He never sends pictures.

He has always had long hair.

I wish I could defend Sam, but right now, I feel ignored and hurt. He should have called. Or e-mailed. He should have told Mom he was finally cutting his hair. He should have wanted to talk to me about the card. And Mac. But complaining won't change anything. "Maybe he'll write again in a few days. When this fire is out. When he is back on base." I don't know if I'm trying to convince myself or Dad. I don't think either one of us believes me.

Dad scurries around the kitchen. "Nothing better than baked apples on a crisp fall day. Any luck talking to Mac?"

Funny how he sneaks *that* in. "No."

"Not even a little?"

"Not even a little."

"Are you sure?"

"I'm sure." Even if I have to eat lunch alone for the rest of the year, I'm not talking to Mac until he returns Wayne Timcoe.

Dad arranges a large tray of apples. Keys jingle in the door. It is Mom, of course, and she's wearing brand-new scrubs, which means she had to change at work, she was that bloody. She drops her purse on the floor and throws a magazine on the table. We must look absolutely morose, because she immediately freaks out. "What's wrong? Has something happened to Sam?"

She is trained to assume the worst.

"We got an e-mail," I say as cheerfully as possible.

"A short one," Dad says. Glum.

It should take five seconds to read, but she stares at the message for at least forty-five.

I say, "I know it's short, but the good news is, he's fine. Just busy. I bet he'll call this Monday."

She scratches her head. "Did you see the pictures?" I ask. "He cut his hair. Just like you asked him to."

Her frown lines deepen. "Ten days of nothing and this is what he sends? No time to write, I'm fine? Here's my picture. Fight to the end for what's important to you? What does that even mean?"

Dad rubs her neck. "I know. I'm frustrated too. I wish he wrote more."

She slams the laptop shut. "Why doesn't he understand that all we want is for him to be—"

"A doctor?" I ask. "Mom, he doesn't want to go to med school. Why can't you get off his back?" I run upstairs to Sam's room and slam the door, so they know exactly how I feel.

The yellow walls, the blue and white bedspread, the collage of pictures all over his door. His varsity letters. His favorite photos: the team, the mountains, a close-up of a soccer ball. His high school jersey. His words.

When Sam was in high school, my parents let him

write his favorite sayings all over the walls in permanent marker. Or maybe, he did it, and they were too lazy to paint over it.

Winning isn't everything . . . it's the only thing.

Trust your gut. Don't be a wuss.

No fear.

It was a whole lot easier being a wuss.

I go to my room and do ten push-ups, then stop. At this point, what's the difference? My parents are mad, and I don't have my card. My brother can't bother to call me, and my oldest friend is a traitor. Maybe they're all in this together. The Wayne Timcoe of the poster looks down at me with confidence. I count to Andrew Jackson, then stop.

Counting presidents is pointless.

Sam was wrong. Fighting to the end does not feel good.

Dad knocks and comes in. I stare at my new goal-keeper's gloves, which claim to feature state-of-the-art technology that provides the ultimate in performance and protection.

"Are you okay? Mom didn't mean to snap at you. She's just really tired." He picks up a glove and sits next to me on the bed. "We're going to go to services. You don't have to come, but since you don't have to be at the field early, I think your mom would appreciate it."

In other words—put on a tie—you're going. Brush your hair. Apologize to your mother. We let you out of services for all your morning games. He says, "If you like, we could say the healing prayer for Sam."

"He doesn't need healing." I look away. I do not want to tempt fate. But I can't help it. "Does he?"

He squeezes my shoulder. "No, but it couldn't hurt. And it might make us feel like we're doing something to help him." I escape his grasp and go to the window.

Outside, it looks like it's going to be a perfect day. There are no visible crows or spiders or even dead bugs. The truth is, I am afraid for Sam too. "What if Sam was counting on me and Wayne Timcoe to give him luck?"

"Oh, Ari." He gets up and stands behind me, and I am grateful that he doesn't want to face me, eye to eye. "Sam's job does not depend on your card. And you are not responsible for anyone's actions but your own. If Sam knew what was going on, he would tell you it was just too bad that Mac isn't a better friend."

We don't move or talk until Mom pops her head in the room. "Are you coming?" she asks in her absolutely nicest, calmest voice.

I want to ask, "Do I have a choice?" but I manage to say, "Sure. It's probably a good idea."

This was obviously the right thing to say. "Thank you, Ari," Dad says. "We'll wait downstairs. Take your time." He gets up and starts to close the door. "Why don't you pack up your gear? We'll go to the game from the Temple. So you will be there in plenty of time."

"Thanks, Dad."

I load my uniform and gear into a bag. I trudge down the stairs. The bag feels heavy. Very heavy.

When we arrive at the synagogue, the service has already started. Everyone is standing and singing and bowing their heads, as the rabbi opens the ark to take out the Torah.

Going to services, when you are studying for your bar mitzvah, is a nerve-racking experience. There are a lot of rituals. And you know you have to learn every single one.

As the rabbi sings, I stare at the words and picture myself standing where he is now. Can I sing that prayer? In Hebrew? At the front of the room? With the Torah on my shoulder? Can I walk around the sanctuary without tripping?

You hear a lot of horror stories. A boy whose voice never stopped cracking—a girl who forgot the entire blessing and started laughing and could not stop. One girl got her shoe caught on a floorboard and almost dropped the Torah, which is, by far, the worst possible most unlucky thing that can happen.

No one drops the Torah. The rabbi once told me that he has never seen one hit the floor.

That is because, if it does, everyone in the room has to fast during the day for forty days.

For the record, if this happens on my bar mitzvah, my father will collapse on the ground and cry, since his lunch will go to waste.

Today, it takes the rabbi five minutes to walk around the room to our seats. Without one bobble, he kisses Mom's cheek and shakes our hands. Impressive. "How is Sam?" he asks. "Any word?"

My mother talks to the rabbi a lot. "He's fine," she says. "We just got a letter from him this morning." A big smile. "We are so proud of him."

Clearly Mom does not tell the rabbi everything.

At the front of the room, the rabbi unwraps the Torah scroll. He says, "Today we will be reading from The Book of Noah." According to him, a hero in his own time, but perhaps not all time.

I have no idea what that means.

As he chants, I daydream about my reading. Maybe the rabbi is right. The team is a responsibility and a burden. I wish I had never asked Mac to give me back my card, and then I wonder if that was my burden, the one the rabbi thinks is supposed to be an honor. At our next meeting, I am going to tell him just how wrong he is.

When the service is over, it is almost noon. We have to go. Even after I ask Mom nicely to hurry up, she kisses every single person in the room. I wait by the door. Eat. Drink. I check the clock four times. I go into the bathroom and change into my uniform. When I open the bathroom door, the rabbi is waiting.

"Nice to see you, Ari," he says. "Big game today?"

Mom has the biggest mouth in the universe. "Not really. Today should be easy. It's just Mooretown."

"Just Mooretown?" The rabbi warns me to play with humility. "Remember the 1950 World Cup? What were the odds? Five hundred to one?"

I almost tell him how happy Mom really was when she got Sam's e-mail. But he'd probably pull out some Torah story about mothers and sons, and I don't have time. It's bad enough when the rabbi wants to combine religion and sports. I don't want to talk about religion, sports, and mothers.

"Yep. Five hundred to one."

A lady walks over to shake his hand. She says, "I feel like I know a whole new side to Noah."

The rabbi smiles. "There is a lot of evidence that he was the first to drink wine."

The lady nods. "But he sure was stubborn. To act that way toward your own son. To disown him, because he was embarrassed? That doesn't seem heroic."

I pretend I was paying attention and that I know what she is talking about. "In the Torah, a lot of sons get a bad deal."

Rabbi never lets you know if he thinks your comment is a dumb one. "So what do you think the Torah is telling us—when a hero can act so carelessly? Even after everything he did, can you still look up to him? Or do our heroes have to be perfect people too?"

I am ninety-nine percent sure he's not talking about Noah anymore. I ask, "What do you think the Torah is saying, Rabbi?"

When talking to a rabbi, answering a question with a question is a great strategy.

"I think the Torah is saying that nobody is perfect, but of course, we should still try to be the best people possible. I think we need to remember that heroes are real people too. They make mistakes."

He is definitely not talking about Noah now.

I motion to Mom. She grabs Dad, and they both shake hands with the rabbi. Mom looks guilty—she definitely said something. Dad looks like he ate too much challah. The rabbi wishes me good luck. He says, "Sometimes, what you expect the least can happen. Sometimes, Ari, the little guy wins against all odds."

Now I really hope he's talking about me.

TWENTY-ONE

"An American tragedy in which we have all played a part."
—Gerald Ford

SOMERSET VALLEY vs. MOORETOWN

MOORETOWN HIGH SCHOOL FIELD
1 P.M.

Unfortunately, there is construction on Main Street. And because construction is not enough to completely stop the flow of traffic and ruin my life, a water main is broken. Even though my father is driving, it takes fifty-two minutes to get to the field. He tells Mom that he will drop us off and come back later, after he stops by the restaurant.

When we arrive, warm-ups are over.

Parker stands in the net. In my net. My spot. She doesn't see me, because she is talking to Eddie. Probably telling him to cover the post. And charge the offense, that they are weak and slow and that this is going to be cake.

Coach is talking to the refs. I run and yell as loud as I can. "Coach! Here I am! I made it."

He meets me at the bench. "Fish! Where have you been? We were about to start without you. It's not like we're in danger of losing to Mooretown, but out of respect, we have to make it look like we're at least a little bit nervous."

"I was at services," I say, putting on the head gear and the mouth guard and counting in my head. *Washington, Adams, Jefferson, Madison, Monroe.* Coach runs toward the goal to tell Parker she's back to warming the bench.

Parker does not look happy. "No hard feelings?" I ask.

She says, "No hard feelings," but her voice is quiet. She does not smile.

I say, "You'll be on the field in no time." I would be disappointed too. Every time Mischelotti took his place in the goal, I thought I would never have my chance.

Her father is mad. He screams at Coach. "Why are you taking my daughter out? Fish was late. She was here. She deserves the opportunity to start in the net. She's done everything you asked her to do. She's twice as good as half the clowns out there."

As I take the field, no one waves hello. Except for Mac, they are all staring at Parker's dad, who is basically freaking out on the sidelines. "It's unfair. It's not right. You don't treat her as an equal. I'm not going to take this lying down. I'm going to report you to the commissioner."

Mac stands at midfield and stretches.

I wonder if everything will ever be normal again, if

we'll ever be able to play together . . . or if the season is shot . . . if we're still even friends. If we'll ever be friends.

I have to do something. If I don't, no one else will.

"Hey Biggs—send it back to me if you need help. Okay? Can we call a truce?" For a second, I'm not sure he heard me.

But then he turns around. "Okay, Ari. Will do." The rest of the defense jogs to the net to shake my hand.

It's a start.

They say, "I'm really glad you made it." And "I thought Mac was going to explode when Coach put Parker in the net." And "He actually complained to Coach."

I want to hear the whole story, but there isn't time. The whistle blows. The game begins. Mooretown takes the ball, but they can't dribble for beans. The lanes shut down. Mooretown is weak and slow, and it doesn't take a genius or even a moderately good athlete to stop them in their tracks. Eddie boots the rock out of our end.

Mac, of course, is everywhere. He weaves around two Mooretown players, traps the ball, and passes it to Soup. It's a perfect pass, and Soup kicks it past the goalkeeper without stumbling or even breaking a sweat.

"Nice job, Campbell!" Coach pumps his fist. A few parents clap politely.

Even Parker can't help showing some enthusiasm.

"Let's do it again!" she yells as Mac steals the ball, if you can call it stealing. From the net, it looks like the Mooretown squad is just watching. Every pass Mac makes is perfect; every shot he takes goes in. "Way to show up, big guy," Coach yells. After ten minutes, Mac scores our fourth goal. Coach opens a lawn chair and sits down.

This might be the most lopsided game in select soccer history.

I'm not complaining, but there's not much for me to do. The ball never reaches the net. Eddie traps it twice, but there is no reason for him to risk kicking anything toward me. This is not Grenada versus Barbados. And Mac is always open.

Mac MacDonald is having the game of his life.

At the end of the period, the score is five to nothing, which is pretty insurmountable, all things considered. Coach gets out of his chair and meets with us in the net. "Now this is what I call fun." He grins the kind of grin people call evil. "If you get stuck, clearly the best thing to do is pass the ball to MacDonald. He's got the hot hand, or should I say, foot." It's an old, silly saying. "That all right with you?" Now he's being sarcastic. Of course it's all right.

I am sure Mac is going to start gloating, but Coach has more to say. "People, I have been at this a long time, and so I can tell when something special is happening. Mark my words: If this season keeps progressing the same way it started, we have a chance to bring home a little precious metal."

I can't help feeling excited. This is my team. I am the keeper. If we are going to do this, we all have to be on the same page.

I put my hand out and hope that somehow, maybe, my luck—even without the card—has begun to turn. Eddie puts his hand on mine. Then Soup. Then David. Mac waits, so his is on the top. For a moment, it feels like everything will go back to normal.

"We can do it," Mac says. "I feel lucky. Beyond lucky. Lucky as the stars. What do you say, Ari? Are you feeling lucky today?"

Jerry Mac MacDonald has always had a lot of nerve, and he is not offering me forgiveness or trust or anything else.

I wait for everyone else to run to the sidelines for water. "Go on, Mac. Say what you want to say. You know I don't feel lucky. At all."

He says, "But you should. Because I know where your card is." His face is serious. "Just look in your girlfriend's backpack." He pats my back, shakes his head, and smiles—just enough so I know he's happy. The winner. The hero. He says, "I promise you, Ari, it's there." Then he starts to walk away.

I don't believe him. "You are a liar."

He looks at me like I am speaking another language. "No I'm not. I never took that card. I never needed it. I never wanted it." He points at Parker, who is sitting on the ground next to her things. "If you had thought about it, you would have realized that only one person wanted what you had. And that person wasn't me. It was Parker."

I lose it.

Big time.

"I don't believe you. Parker did not take it. You're just trying to play with my head."

I aim my fist for his top lip. I want to be Teddy Roosevelt in 1884, who was the only president to give anyone a knuckle sandwich. I swing as hard as I can.

It is a brave moment, perhaps my bravest, but even with two seconds of hindsight, I should have considered a few vital, never-changing facts:

Throwing a punch in the middle of a regulation game is not a smart move, whether the person you are aiming for is your oldest friend or not.

If you land a punch, there is the temporary satisfaction of having successfully pounded your enemy. But Coach's rule: You are out of the game. If you miss, you're done too.

Either way, you have to wait for him to hit you or pray that for some reason, a well-meaning adult intercedes fast enough to stop what is inevitably coming.

Mac ducks.

I miss.

Coach is slow. Way too slow.

One last fact: When someone's fist hits you square in the jaw full force, it makes a hammer sound like a thud. It vibrates. But when your head hits the post, it makes no sound whatsoever.

When I see my mother running onto the field, I realize this has to be rock bottom. Things cannot get any worse.

TWENTY-TWO

"Any man worth his salt will stick up for what he believes right, but it takes a slightly better man to acknowledge instantly and without reservation that he is in error."

—Andrew Jackson

You don't know you've been unconscious until after you wake up.

"Ari, can you hear me? How many fingers do I have up?" There are too many voices. Too many questions.

My head is hot. My arms are hot. My legs are hot. My mother pushes everyone else back. "What is today's date? Who was the first president? Who was the only president not to get married?"

She dumps cold water on my face. "Say something, Ari."

Now I sit up. "James Buchanan was the only bachelor president."

Everyone cheers. Everyone, that is, except Coach. You can tell he is fuming mad, because he is pacing three steps up and three steps back. Up and back. Up and back. He makes me dizzy. "Could someone help this knucklehead off the field? Do you think we have to call an ambulance?" When it is clear that I'm going to survive, his concern disappears. "Fish, MacDonald, on the bench. Now."

Eddie helps me up. He lets me lean on his shoulder all the way to the bench.

It is a very long walk.

My mother looks like she wants to deck me too, but for now, she goes into nurse mode. "Sit," she says, pointing to Coach's lawn chair. That chair is normally off limits, but right now, that is the least of my problems. She grabs cherry-smelling ice and wraps it in a towel around my head. "How is your vision? Your jaw? Any numbness or tingling?" Even though I tell her that I'm fine, she calls my father to come get us immediately.

Coach looks at Mac with disgust. "Whatever you did to set off Fish, I'm not going to tolerate it. Sit on the bench. I'll let you know in a few minutes how generous I'm feeling." Then he looks at me, and his expression does not change. "Fish, you're done for the day." He holds up his hand toward the refs, as in *give me a few more minutes*. "Mischelotti, make sure these clowns don't cause any more trouble."

Mac starts to protest, but Coach won't listen. "I want to see both of you tomorrow. I don't care what you had planned." He gathers our team together and shouts directions. "Llewellyn, go get your gear. I'm putting you in the net."

Mac can't sit still and he won't shut up. "He can't put her in the net. What's wrong with Biggs?"

When Parker takes the field, her dad runs to the south end and yells directions. "Keep your eyes open. Stay alert—they're going to challenge you."

It's extremely good advice.

Mac kicks the bench. "This is all her fault." He whistles to our teammates and my ears feel like they are literally going to explode. When they turn around, he holds up his hand. He makes an *L* with his fingers.

My brain is not completely cloudy. Plan Freeze-out. They're going to go through with it.

I wonder if maybe Mac broke my jaw. "It's not worth it," I say, but Mac won't listen—it's like he's stuck in a horror movie and he doesn't realize that if he just does the smart thing and calls the authorities, everyone will live.

I am not a fan of horror, because it is so predictable.

I start to stand up to talk to Coach, but my mother stops me cold. She wraps a fresh towel and ice around my head. "You are not allowed to move. Not one step until your father gets here with the car. Do you understand?"

I understand.

Her cell phone rings. It is extremely loud. Mac says, "Cool your jets. I have no intention of forfeiting this game. We just have to prove to Coach that he can't put her in the net. It won't take long. He'll get the picture."

Moorctown takes the ball straight down the field toward our goal. Mischelotti won't leave me alone.

"Fish, you look like a swami. Want to tell my fortune?"

This is a disaster.

David trips on the sideline. Eddie misses an easy interception. Our friends may be able to play, but they cannot act. It's totally obvious. I need to warn her. Parker Llewellyn is playing alone. She is the only person on our team who is trying.

She grabs the ball and sends a nice kick to midfield. Normally, Soup would have this, no problem. Today, he gets in front of it. I think maybe he changed his mind, and everything will work out, but of course, this is a horror movie, so he stumbles right into the biggest Mooretown player. The ball bounces to their forwards. Mischelotti yawns. "I thought they were better than this."

"They *are* better than this."

We watch Mooretown approach the net. Parker shouts at Eddie to help her cover the left side, but he steps forward, too close to midfield, totally out of position.

Mr. Llewellyn yells, "That's not in the playbook. Get back in position. Show some hustle."

Parker saves another uncontested shot. Mischelotti says, "You know, MacDonald, she's gotten pretty good. Look at the way she moves laterally. She's really not bad."

"Shut up," Mac says.

Mischelotti does not shut up. "What do you have against her anyway?"

"I don't have anything against her. I just don't want her playing on my team."

"Yeah right." Mischelotti laughs. "If you cared so much about your precious team, you'd see—that girl is good. You are better with her than without her." We watch her stop another shot on goal. "I don't think I'd do any better."

I don't think I would either.

But no one can do it alone.

After four more minutes, Parker comes out of the net too far. She acts too much like a field defender. Then she goes for a fake. No surprise. It's her first game, and she can't help making rookie mistakes.

When Mooretown scores, Mac smirks. He stands up and waves to Coach. He prepares to enter the game.

Coach does nothing. He does not signal to Mac. He does not call his number.

Mooretown drives downfield again and again and again. I shout as loud as my brain will allow, "Stay in the net. Keep your eyes on the feet. Don't trust your teammates—they are hanging you out to dry."

But I think she has figured that out.

"Tell them to play," I beg Mac. I spit blood. One of my fake teeth is loose. I feel like I am going to throw up. Even talking makes my head throb. The lead is down to two.

But Mac won't let it go. "She stole your card. Just ask her. I dare you."

Mischelotti gets up and sits between us. "You guys are such babies. This would never happen on our lacrosse team."

Mac says, "I don't see any girls infiltrating your lacrosse team. And we will not lose. As soon as Coach can, he'll put me in and everything will be fine."

Ten minutes later, Mooretown ties the game, and Parker's dad runs past us screaming, "What is the matter with you? Why aren't you helping her?"

I don't believe this. "Mac, please. This isn't funny. Tell Coach now. Before it's too late."

Mac points to her bag. "I will if you look in her bag."

Mischelotti says, "Go for it, Swami. Check her backpack. No one's looking."

I shake my head. "No."

My mom finally returns. She takes the towel off my head and checks my mouth. She whispers, "Do you want me to go get Coach?"

I nod.

Get him.

I hope it's not too late.

By the time Mom has cornered Coach, Mooretown is up by one. He walks to our side of the field. And even though he says the whole thing feels and smells fishy, he relents. "Go in, MacDonald. But if you think I'm taking her out, think again."

Mac doesn't mouth off. He doesn't demand that Coach bench Parker. He knows this is a moment made for a hero.

As planned, the entire team responds. Soup blocks the inbound throw, and passes the ball to Mac, who needs only thirty or so seconds to score, no assist necessary. For a moment, I relax. It is over. Tie game. We'll win in overtime. No harm done.

But I have forgotten some of the biggest truths about soccer. Momentum can beat skill. Any team can score on any given day.

The rabbi is right—a weak team can beat a strong one.

Now that Mooretown feels confident, they play strong. They attack Mac, who is still not in his rhythm. Even though I know my team is finally trying to win, Mooretown weaves in and out and around us, no sweat.

The final sequence could be called righteous soccer, and it is right out of the youth soccer handbook.

They dribble down the lane, then pass across the field. Practically everyone on the offense touches the ball.

It's not like we aren't trying.

Mac tries to steal the ball, but good teamwork trumps one good player any day. He isn't warmed up, and his legs look slow and stiff. Around midfield, he trips and falls. He can only watch their center take his shot.

It's a good kick. High and solid. A bullet to the corner. No luck involved.

We lose seven goals to six.

I couldn't have stopped it either.

When everyone has congratulated Mooretown, Coach speaks softly, which is how we know he is really, really mad. "You played slow and careless. Intentionally sloppy.

Llewellyn was the only one playing, and don't think I don't know it." He squeezes her shoulder. "I thought you understood—there is no *I* in team."

After a bad loss, there is nothing more pathetic than the *I*-in-team speech.

Coach says, "I never thought I would coach a team that would intentionally go out and lose."

Mac raises his hand. "Coach, this is my fault," he says. "I told them to quit, but I didn't want to lose. I really thought in the end, we would win."

My head pounds. This is Mac's fault, Mac's plan, but it is my fault too. I should have said something. I could have helped Parker. I could have stood up with her, instead of focusing only on myself and my card.

Soup kicks a patch of dirt. He won't look at anyone, and David Old starts rubbing his eyes, and I don't think he's faking. Eddie shakes his head. "You promised us it would work."

Mac doesn't disagree. "You're right, Biggs. I feel like a jerk. This loss is on me."

I would not be surprised if smoke came out of Coach's ears. He starts then stops then paces a few more steps. He sends the parents to the parking lot. "If you don't mind, I'd like a few minutes alone with the team." Everyone leaves except Parker's dad, who uses the moment to tell all of us that he has played on a lot of teams, but never one as horrible as this.

When he has nothing left to say, it is so quiet, I can

hear birds. They sound anxious, but they're probably not. They're probably just being birds.

Coach says, "You embarrassed me. You embarrassed yourselves. I have half a mind to forfeit the rest of the season."

Everyone talks at once. I hear a lot of *no*'s. And *you can't*s. A few people are brave enough to admit, "We didn't think it would take so long to put Mac back in."

When Parker stands up, everyone is quiet again. "Please don't do it," she says. "Not now. Not for me. I don't think it really is about me. If we just talk this out and get Ari his card, everything will work out."

Girls. Even after everything that happened, she still thinks talking is the answer. Her father looks like he agrees with me. "I disagree," he says. "They let you down. You don't have to be nice."

"No. She's right," Mac says. "I told everyone to stop playing because she told Ari I had the card. And for some reason, he believed her."

Now everyone nods. They say things like "That's right." And "It was a spur of the moment thing. It got totally out of hand."

My head pounds. My ears ring. But my feet feel steady, and I know a lie when I hear one. "You made this plan weeks ago. We were all there."

Now it is so quiet, I can hear air.

Parker walks toward me, and I hold up my hand—to protect my jaw. That's how mad she looks.

"You knew?" When she starts to cry, her dad runs back to the group. "You knew they were going to quit on me and you didn't say anything?"

Pain shoots from my neck, through my shoulder, to my hand. "I never thought they'd actually do it."

Mac seems to perk up. He steps between me and Parker. "Come on, Parker, give the guy a break. The guy took a swing at me. He got benched because I told him about your little secret."

Now Parker looks sick. And guilty. She stares at the grass. A bad sign. "My secret?"

"Yeah." Mac says. "Your secret. And now it's time for you to confess." Mac always smiles just before he takes a shot. "You've got Ari's Wayne Timcoe card. Admit it."

Parker drops her stuff. She looks at Mac and shakes her head. "Ari, do you honestly believe I'd steal your card?"

Honestly?

Mac says, "Me and Soup saw you looking at it. You stuck it in your backpack. We could tell you didn't want anyone to see what you were doing."

Soup nods to me. "It's true. He's not lying. She was definitely hiding something."

Now she looks mad and sad. "No," she says. "I don't have it. I swear. Coach, they don't know what they saw." She buries her head in her father's chest while he kisses the top of her head. I can hear her whimper, "This is so embarrassing."

Mac sneers. "Because you're a liar and a thief?"

When she turns around, I wouldn't want to be Mac. "If you have to know, MacDonald, I was getting . . . you know . . ." She turns red. "Girl things."

Oh.

That.

Everyone groans.

Parker's dad claps his hands. "Okay, then, that's enough. You boys have acted badly enough for one day. Let's go, Parker."

Coach agrees. "Go home. We'll have a team meeting after school on Monday."

But Mac won't let anyone move. He says, "No. She can't get away with this. She framed me! She stole Ari's card!"

Parker picks up her bag and clutches it to her chest. Her dad asks, "Do you have it, sweetheart? Because if you do, and you still want to be part of this team, you have to give it back. Now."

She pulls away. "If it's there, he planted it."

Mac shakes his head. "I knew she'd say that."

I want to believe her. I want to believe her more than I want to believe Mac. But realistically, I'm not sure. A lot of things don't make sense. She is the only other collector here. She's the only person I know still looking for a Timcoe. She was the only person who saw Mac go into my stuff.

Mac is my friend. She hates Mac. She practically said so herself.

Her father grabs the bag, and she starts to protest. "It's the only way you're going to earn their respect." He unzips the front flap.

She says, "Don't!"

He shakes the bag hard. Out fall a sweatshirt and a bottle of water, an extra shirt, a notebook. A pink pouch. A small stuffed dog.

And half a dozen All-Star Soccer trading cards.

I don't want to look. She says, "Daddy, I swear, those cards are not mine."

Mac says, "You got that right."

I look. But only to convince myself. There is no way my card is in her backpack. Mac is wrong. It's the only thing that makes sense.

Until I look at her face and see that she is scared. She is scared of me. And the cards. Scattered on the ground.

One by one, I pick them up. They are all classics, all well cared for. Just like the day in front of Ben Elliot's, I know before I see him.

First blue. Then red. A bright green field.

There is nothing worse than being lied to.

Parker picks up the card, before I have to bend over to get it. She hands it to me, like it is hot enough to burn. "He put it there, Ari. You have to believe me. He planned this. You know he did. You know I would never take him away from you."

I don't kiss it.

I don't rub it on my leg.

I don't let anyone else touch it.

It is Wayne, Wayne Timcoe, my trading card, my lucky card, in a custom plastic sleeve, the kind that costs two for three dollars, the kind that only real collectors buy.

Everyone leaves, heads down, eyes on the grass. There really isn't much to say. Dad finally shows up and he and Mom take me by my elbows and help me to the car. "Ari, what happened?"

I tell him everything—who hit whom and Parker having the card. He *tsks*. "Well, I'm surprised. She seemed like a nice girl."

Mom says, "Maybe too nice. You know, I never could believe that Mac was guilty." She makes a pillow out of a sweatshirt that smells like tomato sauce. "Mac has been your friend for a long time. And I hope now you two can figure things out." When I yawn a second time, she goes ballistic. "Are you sleepy? Can you please stay awake?" Although the motion of the car is very relaxing, her voice is not. She says three times, "I bet he has a concussion." Every time I close my eyes, she complains about Coach and my friends and even my obsession with Wayne.

I hold the card. He is so perfect. I ask, "Do you think Mac's telling the truth? That she framed him?"

Dad hits a pothole. Mom tells him to be more careful.

I say, "Parker knew the card was lucky."

Mom hands me a water bottle. Dad asks, "Why don't you stop worrying about who took it, and just be grateful you have it back? Remember, everyone makes mistakes. Parker was under a lot of pressure."

My father, the king of the underdogs.

"So was I. So was Mac." Dad drives. I sulk. Possession is nine-tenths of the law. "The whole time, she was the one who thought the card was so cool. She was also the one who made me believe he had it. The whole time, she was the only person who saw him take it."

I examine the card for nicks or damages. Stains. The plastic cover is nice. It is obviously new. A few smudges, but otherwise, pristine. It's obvious a collector took care of this card.

The rest of the way, the only thing they say is, "Stay awake, Ari." Dad doesn't complain about leaving work. He doesn't worry (out loud) how much my tooth will cost. Mom stops telling him how to drive. I keep my eyes open.

"Stay awake, Ari."

As soon as we get to the emergency room, Mom jumps out of the car. A wheelchair and half the nurses she works with are waiting. It takes them an hour to declare me healthy and in one piece.

Before we go, the doctor gives me a new ice pack and tells me to take something for the pain. He says to Mom, "Take tonight off. Wake him up every four hours, just to be safe. And get some sleep. I can't believe you're still standing."

TWENTY-THREE

"I feel incompetent to perform duties . . . which have been so unexpectedly thrown upon me."

—Andrew Johnson

At home, Dad makes coffee. Mom puts up her feet. The painkillers let pain live. If I move, my entire mouth throbs.

The newspaper sits folded on the table. Steve the Sports Guy tells Sick of Being Nagged to get off the couch and confront his girlfriend. And Frustrated About Work needs a new job. I'm surprised when he thinks the Galaxy fan who doesn't want to read about the Lakers is overreacting to her daughter's boyfriend. Usually, he tells people to trust their guts. But this time, he advises the guy to "Sit back. Wait and see. Maybe the kid is sincere. Maybe he isn't. Just love your daughter. Time will tell."

The phone rings. Mom answers. "It's Parker. Are you available?"

"No."

I don't want to fight. I don't want to hear any excuses. I only get out of bed to e-mail Sam. "We lost," I write. "Everything is falling apart."

She calls three more times in the first hour. Two times in the next. The last time, Mom says, "She sounds really sad."

"I said no."

I'm not talking. I'm not listening. I don't care—I don't feel like doing the right thing.

Even though it doesn't feel very good.

The next day, right before dinner, Coach stops by with Mac. "I don't care how things got out of hand," he says, "but now I want you to make it go away."

Mac goes first. "I guess I really let Parker get to me." He puts out his hand to shake mine. "I guess I let a lot of things get to me. It made me mad, when you blamed me for your lost card. We are friends. Teammates. I couldn't believe you thought I could do something like that to you."

If I were honest, I would say:

If you didn't take it, why didn't you just tell me? Why did you act so guilty?

You're not playing this straight. You never gave her a chance.

How about an apology?

But I am not honest. Coach is here. He doesn't look like he wants to actually talk about what happened. He expects me to accept whatever it is Mac is offering and move on for the sake of the team.

So even though nothing has been resolved, that is what I am going to do. I try to think of something to say.

Something honest. Something that will get them out of my house.

"I'm just glad I have the card again."

Mac says, "You know, All-Star Soccer says that Wayne Timcoe card is worth two thousand dollars. You were really lucky to get it back before Parker tried to unload it."

He does not understand the first thing about collecting. "Since when did you care about the value of trading cards? I thought you said the cards were worthless."

It is an extremely awkward moment.

Coach clears his throat. "Ari, give your friend a break. I don't think Mac was suggesting that you should sell the Timcoe. I don't think he believes it is worthless."

Mac jumps all over that. "I don't. I know how much that card means to you. I'm glad you got it back." We stare at each other in silence until he blinks. "This has been the worst week of my life. I want to put this entire chapter behind us."

When I don't immediately chime in, Coach frowns. He thinks I'm stalling. "Ari, Mac is reaching out to you." In other words, say something. Do the right thing. Shake hands and make up, so we can get back to work.

So I shake Mac's hand. When he hugs me, I hug back. And for Coach, this means that the conflict is over. "Good. I'm glad we had this little talk."

They are about to leave, when Dad brings out a pot full of chili with side dishes of cheese and very soft for-a-sore-jaw tortillas. Coach looks at his watch, tells us he needs to go, but he will stay a bit longer for some comfort food this tasty.

Mac and I eat three servings each. Coach stops at two. "Boys, if this team is going to succeed, you two are going to have to put all this behind you. You're going to have to play together. You're going to have to find a way to—"

"We know."

Mac takes the last of the tortillas, but leaves the last scoop of cheese for me. He promises he'll lead the team to victory. He'll even get Mischelotti off my back. "I know I've been a total jerk. That whole scene in the cafeteria was not right. But trust me—I am going to make it up to you."

I burp. Too many hot peppers. "Are you actually apologizing to me, Mac MacDonald?"

He burps too. A little one. "Yes. I'm sorry." We each grab a bottle of soda and chug all the way until there's nothing left. It is easy to believe Mac. It's fun to be his friend. We take turns burping—each time, a little bit louder—until Mac lays a loud, long one, and I give up. Then we both start laughing and I hiccup a bunch of times, so hard it hurts. Mac says, "I never want to drive anywhere with Mischelotti again. His car stinks!" And I say, "And I never want to hear the Mia Hamm story again."

Coach leaves the room to talk to Dad. Mac shakes my hand again. There are no jokes. No one is listening. He says, "I know I haven't always been the best friend, and

I'm sorry about that. I'm really glad this is over. I hope you will be able to trust me again."

Trust is a big deal.

It's the key ingredient of a team. You have to trust that your teammates have your back. You have to trust that everyone is playing their best.

Most of all, you have to trust that they won't lie to your face.

Parker trusted us to play, but she shouldn't have. I trusted her with the card, but then she stole it. Now Mac wants me to trust him.

I want to believe him, but something doesn't feel right. "You're my striker. We have to stick together." I don't think that is exactly what he wanted to hear, but right now, it's the best I can do.

Coach makes us promise to be fair to Parker. "She may have done something terrible, but we're a team, and that means you're not allowed to hold it against her." He says he is too old for this nonsense, but it is obvious he believes Mac. "It will be rough at first. There will be some bumps. But I won't lead a team that can't play together."

We shake hands one more time. It's a deal.

After they leave, when I am alone in my room, when Mom isn't asking me if my mouth is still sore and Dad isn't worrying that the next shipment of grass-fed beef is going to be late, and I'm not worried that Sam still hasn't returned any of my desperate, urgent e-mails, I secretly can't help feeling a little bit of doubt.

The truth is Parker could have framed Mac. But Mac could have framed Parker too. If it hadn't been for him, we never would have lost that game.

But then I remember what the rabbi said right before the game. About Noah. And heroes.

Nobody's perfect.

Heroes are just people.

We all make mistakes.

In the early morning, the sun turns the sky from red to pink to a misty blue-gray haze. Behind some clouds, the sun is a white-yellow ball.

But something is off. The sky looks strange. It takes me a few minutes to figure it out.

Even though the sky is light enough for me to see the red leaves on the trees, I can see the moon. It looks like it is made of dust, a shadow of the big yellow sun, determined to stick around.

But there it is. The moon. During the day.

It looks a little unreal, a little off balance, like the whole world is out of whack.

Not just me.

TWENTY-FOUR

*"A president's hardest task is not to do what is right,
but to know what is right."*

—Lyndon B. Johnson

Optimism: take one.

I get out of bed and do my push-ups. I recite the presidents with the highest approval ratings. Even though my jaw, shoulder, and arm ache, I have the card. I hold Wayne Timcoe in both hands, look at the poster, and hope for good things for myself. And Sam. And Mac. And Parker too. The weekend is past. The correlation between the card and luck is still predictable: When I have the card, I play well. Girls talk to me. Everything is great.

On my way to the bathroom, I stub my toe.

Maybe the card just needs some time to warm up.

Optimism: take two.

I check my e-mail. There are ten messages in my inbox. One is from Sam.

> Got your messages. Sorry to hear things have
> been tough. Let's talk about it tonight.

He will call tonight—that's good. But he forgot to write: "Fight to the end for what's important to you."

He never leaves that out. I'm absolutely positive that it doesn't mean anything. It's just a slogan. Maybe he is trying to come up with a new one.

I print the new message and fold it around the Wayne Timcoe card.

The next e-mail is from Coach. It is marked *urgent* with a bright red exclamation point. I don't have to open it to know what he wants.

On Monday, we're having a special mandatory practice. No whining. No excuses. No slack. He writes, "After what happened at Mooretown, you'll be lucky if you get out of here before dinner."

The other eight messages are from Parker. Pretty much, each message is the same, except the last four are all in capital letters.

> BELIEVE ME. I DID NOT STEAL YOUR WAYNE
> TIMCOE CARD. MAC IS A LIAR. THERE IS
> NO WAY I WOULD STEAL SOMETHING AS
> IMPORTANT AS WAYNE, NOT IN A MILLION
> TRILLION YEARS.

Abraham Lincoln said, "You can fool some of the people all of the time, and all of the people some of the time, but you cannot fool all of the people all of the time."

I wish Lincoln had said something about doubt and overcoming it. I wish he had said something about what you're supposed to be if you don't want to be that fool. Because there is something about her messages that is extremely disturbing.

Optimism: take three.

The newspaper arrives on time.

But my horoscope is grim.

"It's not the best time to make big decisions, as you're swimming in too much data and need to prune some of it away first. Try to put off anything big for a while and then you'll be fine."

No fooling.

The rest of the paper is no better. On the second page: "Helicopter Crash Kills Four in Oregon." Four would-be firefighters are dead. Mark, Tim, Evan, and Sal. Mark was the pilot. Sal was training to be a jumper.

I show Dad, and he starts writing letters.

Dear Mr. and Mrs. Morrison,

My family would like to express our gratitude . . .

When he is done, he asks, "Will you sign these cards? I want to put them in the mail today."

Usually, I just sign my name. But today, I write at the

bottom of each card: "Your son will be missed. We are sorry for your loss."

The morning continues to worsen. We are all out of my before-practice cereal. The only milk left is skim. Dad offers to make pancakes, which sounds great, but then he burns the first two batches. The smoke detector rings like a siren. He hands me a placemat. The Battle of Chickamauga. The next batch are only burnt in random places, so we eat them anyway, even the black parts. Mom reminds me that if my head aches, I should go directly to the nurse.

She says, "Make me proud." That means "Make up with Parker." And "Really forgive Mac."

I can't help wondering if Mac is telling the truth.

Instead of commiserating, Dad sighs. "I don't think it matters. Because no matter what, you are going to do the right thing."

This sounds familiar. "Did you talk to the rabbi too?"

It is obvious he did, but he will never admit it. The last pancake is deformed, a fold-over, and it looks a little like the state of Texas, the home state of Lyndon B. Johnson and Dwight Eisenhower. He answers my question with a question. "Do you think any of the presidents ever hesitated from doing what they thought was right?"

I pour more syrup on the plate. "But what if it doesn't work? What if it's too late?"

Dad kisses the top of my head. "Then at least you tried."

• • •

When I walk out the door, my resolve is strong. Dad is right. I need to do the right thing. I can forget all about the past and who did what and bring my team together. It is not going to be that hard. Mac is already on board. All we have to do is tell everyone—including Parker— that we are all square. No more debate. Then we'll all go to practice and everything will be fine.

Halfway to school, I know exactly what I want to say. But when I arrive, everyone is so happy to see me. It doesn't feel right to make a big, difficult speech.

I convince myself that I don't have to say anything. Everything is already fine. My luck is returning. There is no burden to lift. The power of the card is going to solve all my problems, no sweat.

I ignore the funny little shots my friends take at Parker, Eddie's eye roll and Soup's dead gaze when she arrives at school. I tell myself it means nothing—that old habits die hard and nothing more. Besides, Parker doesn't say hello to us either. She stays on her side of the lawn until the bell rings, and when we walk in her direction, she runs ahead. I say to Mac, "Let's go catch up with her now." He says we don't have to anymore—the deal is off. Parker is quitting—he heard through the grapevine. He reminds me that that proves she is guilty.

I ignore that icky feeling in my gut.

"Are you sure?"

"I'm sure."

I plan to talk to her at lunch. Or maybe after school or

on the way to practice, if Mac's rumor is false. Although I promised to be nice to her, I didn't say that I would resolve everything first thing.

I rationalize that I can actually be more effective if I wait for the card to come to full strength. I don't need to make a big stink, or rock the boat, if I stand back and let the card work its magic.

In other words, I take the easy way out.

I say and do absolutely nothing.

Unfortunately for me, a girl who plays on a boys' team never forgets what she has set out to do. She does not put off until tomorrow what she can do right now.

Right before lunch, she barricades my locker. "You have to talk to me sometime. Why didn't you answer my e-mails? I know you got them."

A second ago I was hungry and happy. Now I feel sick. Guilty. Awful. Trapped again. An hour ago I knew exactly what to do. Now when my mouth opens, out comes, "I don't know what you want me to say."

"Are you serious?" She stamps her foot. "Do you not remember that I was the one trying to help you? Who stuck up for you, when all your so-called-friends were acting like jerks?"

"I remember."

Parker Llewellyn is upset. She stands very stiff. She makes sure everyone in the vicinity can hear. "I called you all weekend long, and your mother said you couldn't talk, which I know is a lie, but what am I supposed to do, call your mother a liar?"

I am so frustrated. At her. At Mac. At this card that seems to have lost all its power. I want to say "I believe you." Or "I forgive you." But she won't stop yelling.

I can yell too. "But it was in your bag."

"He framed me."

"He says you are quitting."

"Well, now we know he's a liar."

I open my locker and it smells like garlic. Everything is wet. It is my hummus sandwich. I must not have sealed the bag, because it is leaking all over everything.

I say, "Everything stinks." I almost shout, "Wayne Timcoe, where are you? I am supposed to be lucky."

As it is, Parker is laughing at me. "Your lunch is peeing."

This is the worst day ever.

"It's not funny." At some moment—any time now—the card is going to start working. My luck is going to start getting better and it's going to stay good. And then it's going to become great, and I will say the right thing, and everyone will get along. I won't have to feel stuck in the middle.

My jacket will stink all day. I pull out the lunch bag. I hope the cookies are wrapped in plastic.

They're not.

For a second, Parker looks me right in the eye, and she doesn't blink. Her voice is finally quiet. "Ari. Just listen. I would never do this, and I'm not going anywhere until you believe me."

I want to tell her that I believe her too, but Mac is here. He and Soup and Eddie are standing behind her. They wave to me and bat their eyes.

She doesn't see them. "Just think about it," she says. "Logically. Why would I ever do that to you?"

Mac taps her on the shoulder. "Because you wanted what he had," he says. "That's why."

Eddie looks embarrassed. Soup turns away. Mac looks like he is offended when she glares at him. He asks, "You coming to lunch, Fish?"

I want to go. I want to stay. I want to tell Mac he is acting like an idiot, that we promised Coach we would be nice to Parker, who, until further notice, is still our teammate. I want to do what Sam and Dad would do. Mom said, "Make me proud." Dad said, "Do the right thing." Sam would probably say "This is important."

That is harder than it sounds. "Please, Parker, everyone wants you to stay on the team. Everything is forgotten."

"Forgotten?" Her lower lip quivers. "What do you mean?"

I stand there like an idiot.

Her eyes change to slits. Her brow furrows. "No it isn't. Not even close." She steps aside—no sign of tears. "You know what I think? That card is evil. Or cursed. I don't know. Maybe you're cursed too."

Now I'm mad. And when I'm mad, I say stupid things. Hurtful things. "The card is not evil. It's the best card I have, and you wanted it." I slam my locker shut. She flinches. "You're just jealous because your footwork is too slow. You're not big enough or strong enough and you're not going to get recruited by anyone until you step up your game. If you and your dad could have accepted that, maybe the team would have accepted you."

I don't really think any of this is true. But I'm mad, and it feels good to make her feel terrible.

For a second.

Then it feels awful. Everything has snowballed out of control. I don't believe anything I've just said.

Before I can take it back, Parker walks away. My friends surround me and congratulate me for finally dealing with that lying, thieving, friend-destroying wanna-be.

Mac puts his arm around my shoulder. Even Eddie looks relaxed. Mac says, "You did the right thing, Fish. We are a great team."

It is the biggest lie yet, but still, I don't look back.

TWENTY-FIVE

"Competition has been shown to be useful up to a certain point and no further, but cooperation, which is the thing we must strive for today, begins where competition leaves off."

—Franklin D. Roosevelt

At the special mandatory practice, Coach says, "There's only one way to get through a crisis like this, and that is hard work."

He's not joking.

First he makes us run to the top of the field and back as fast as we can. When we're done, he says, "Do it again."

And again.

And again.

He does not care how tired we feel, or how lousy we look. He doesn't let us stop running for a drink or a snack or to ease up on a cramp.

Or to ice a sore mouth.

"Coach," Mac says, "this is brutal."

"You don't like it?" He laughs. "Take an extra lap. Or

don't bother coming back." He tells us that this is how practices are going to be until we start acting like a team. We are going to do things his way for as long as it takes. "Do you understand?"

We understand.

We are all miserable.

He lines us up, and we do push-ups, planks, and sit-ups until we can't move. Then he yells, "Get up," and we dribble around the cones.

Three times.

Parker is the only one not gasping for breath. She runs the best average time. And she doesn't knock down a single cone. She glares at me. "You think Coach will have any problem playing me now?"

Then Coach shortens the field by half. He divides us into teams, and we scrimmage six on six, which puts twice as much pressure on the defense.

No one likes playing on a short field. Not Eddie. Not Mac. Not me. I tell Eddie to just take the corner or stay in front of me, and he does not appreciate my advice. Parker is everywhere. She dribbles between defenders and passes with perfect accuracy.

It is extremely aggravating.

Soup yells at Mac. Mac insults David. Eddie starts to yell at me, but I tell him not to start. Even though this is only a scrimmage, I hate scooping out balls from the back of the net.

But it is still not enough for Coach. When we're done,

he shortens the field even more. "Let's play two on two," he says while pacing in front of us. Mac smells. So do I. We smell so bad, I want to step away.

"Up first: MacDonald and Llewellyn against Fish and Biggs."

For a moment, Mac forgets his promises. "Come on, Coach. Can't you play someone else?" He lays on the charm. "All things considered."

Coach isn't buying. He says, "All things considered, MacDonald, you are lucky that any of us will tolerate your presence on this field." He paces back and forth. "Team, I want to win games. I will do anything to win games. And that means playing with the best we have. I know you don't want to believe this, MacDonald, but we need Llewellyn. She is good. I've been watching her close, and this Saturday, she's going to see real time. On offense. Do you hear me, MacDonald?"

"Yes."

Usually, Mac can talk anyone into anything. But not today. Today of all days, Coach decides that Mac does not know what is best for our team.

He says, "So if you want to play on Saturday, get out there and play. Together."

Parker seizes the moment and runs onto the field. "I'm ready." She looks at me and Mac. "Are you?"

What happens next is not pretty.

Coach sends us to the field, two on two, offense on

defense, Mac and Parker against me and Eddie.

Eddie tries to force the ball wide—to keep them from passing—but he is out of position. Too aggressive. Mac has no problem getting the ball to Parker. She dribbles tight. Her feet are super-fast. Left and right and right-left-left-right, and smash—into the corner.

I have to dive headfirst to get it.

That really hurts.

After ten minutes, she scores twice, Mac once. I try and spell it out to Eddie—that he can't just charge the ball, he's got to wait for it—he's got to watch their footwork. That the feet will tell you which way they're going to kick.

He doesn't appreciate it. He tells me he understands watching the feet. And that I should cut him some slack. "You know this drill favors the O." When I don't immediately agree, he adds, "You are becoming a diva."

Mischelotti stands there and shakes his head. "Haven't I taught you anything, Fish? You have to be nice to your stopper."

Eddie doesn't know when to shut up. "At least Parker had a reason to yell. At least she doesn't act like she knows everything, and that everyone else knows squat."

Mischelotti hands me some water. "I thought you guys were friends."

Parker can't help chiming in. "It's because of the stupid card." She says, "I think it's cursed."

He scratches his head. "Maybe it is. Maybe the net is cursed too. Or maybe it's you, Fish. Maybe you're doomed. Just like Wayne Timcoe himself."

I stay up late, overanalyzing everything that has gone wrong.

Sam didn't call, even though he promised he would. I'm sure it only means what it always means. There was another fire. Otherwise, he would have called.

I can't consider anything else.

The non-call has nothing to do with my horrible luck.

And my horrible luck has nothing to do with the card. Or Parker. Or Mac. It's just a coincidence. These things happen. Luck gets better. Then it gets worse. Then it gets better. It is a wave, just like Steve the Sports Guy said. In a couple of days, everything is going to turn around, if not exponentially, at least incrementally.

I believe that.

I have to believe that.

All I have to do is apologize. When I do that, my conscience will feel better. My luck will improve.

What I did was wrong.

I knew Parker loved Wayne just as much as I do, but I never once thought she'd take him. When I realized the card was gone, I did not ever consider that Parker was the thief. Parker was my friend. She is my friend. When no one else would talk to me, she did.

I picture her at the field. At my locker. I remember

what she looked like when she found the card in her backpack. She looked shocked, surprised, upset. I remember how, during tryouts, I was so scared she'd be starting instead of me.

I knew it then. I know it now.

My gut is never wrong.

The door creaks open, and a sliver of brightness cuts the room in half. Dad whispers, "Ari, you're still up?"

My eyes need time to adjust to the light. "I can't sleep."

"Me neither." He closes the door, so the room is dark.

It's a funny thing. I went out of my way to convince myself of the truth, but only in the dark can I say what I fear most. "I wanted to believe that Parker took the card, but now I'm sure she didn't."

He says nothing.

I say, "I was really mean to her."

I can't see Dad's face, but I'm pretty sure he's not smiling. "I'm very sorry to hear that."

I tell him everything.

"You need to apologize," he says.

"But what about Mac?"

My dad lets me think for a very long time. This is his way of making me come up with my own answers. "But what if he won't admit what he did?" I ask.

Dad rubs my head. "Talk to him. Be frank. Tell him you forgive him. He'll come around. There have been plenty of times when he has had to forgive you."

This is true. He has forgiven me a lot.

For the time I gave him a model racecar, then took it back. Same day.

For the time I told the teacher he had copied off my homework.

For the time I told him I had plans, when really, I just didn't feel like hanging out with him.

Me and Mac—we may not always do the right thing— but in the end, we always stick together.

When Dad leaves, he opens the door wide. The hall light shines across my face, like a spotlight. I close my eyes, until it disappears with a click.

Tomorrow, I'm going to do what I should have done before. I am going to talk to Parker. First thing. I'm going to ask for her forgiveness, and then, we're going to talk to Mac. For the first time, I'm going to be a leader. I'm going to do what Thomas Jefferson and Steve the Sports Guy and Sam would tell me to do: I'm going to fight until the end. I'm going to trust my gut. I'm not going to be a wuss anymore.

In the darkness, it feels easy. In the darkness, I am finally ready to do what's right.

At 4:42, the phone wakes me up. Dad's footsteps rush past my door. His voice echoes. Three words. "Hello? What? No."

Downstairs, he is sitting in the dark. His face is in his

hands. The phone is on its side. It beeps steadily, but Dad doesn't touch it.

"What happened?" I ask.

He looks at me with glassy, dazed eyes. "Sam is in trouble."

It's the call we've been dreading.

TWENTY-SIX

"The credit belongs to the man who is actually in the arena, whose face is marred by dust and sweat and blood; who strives valiantly; who errs, who comes short again and again, because there is no effort without error and shortcoming."

—Theodore Roosevelt

"Turn on the news."

Of the seven news stations broadcasting at this hour, none are reporting about the newest fire on the Nevada-California border. It is ten minutes before the hour, which apparently means it is the perfect time to discuss weather and/or entertainment.

Dad calls Sam's cell. When there is no answer, he calls Mom. "Come home." He stares at the commercials, one after the other after the other. He does not flip the channels the way he normally would.

We must wait until exactly 5:07 in the morning for the anchorman to face the camera dead on. A banner appears: FIREFIGHTERS BATTLING MASSIVE BLAZE. MULTIPLE HOMES DESTROYED.

There is no good way to hear bad news.

The anchorman's voice stays steady and low. "In our next story, our thoughts are with a team of firefighters who have been battling another huge blaze near the California-Nevada border."

Mom walks into the room just as the correspondent, a woman named Suzanne Myers, whose super-white hair is blowing around her face, warns parents that the following images may be too frightening for small children to see.

Houses are on fire. The grass is black. A tall tree bursts into flames.

"Paul," she says, "a representative from Redding's Region Five Smokejumpers called in this morning to report that a small fire in this area had been successfully contained. But obviously, something went terribly wrong. Late this evening, the fire re-ignited and blazed out of control. The local fire chief suspects arson."

None of us move.

On the TV, the air is dark. Smoke billows from house after house after house. I wonder where the people are. The firefighters. They should be hosing down these houses, but they aren't.

I don't see any firefighters anywhere.

The reporter's voice shakes. "Right now, more than a dozen men are camped on a ridge in the distance. It was supposed to be a safe zone. But when the fire unexpectedly blew up, it jumped the road and burned through their water supply. It raced up and around that hill."

I try to see the hill. The men. But I can't.

The picture cuts back to Suzanne, who wipes her eyes. She introduces a man in a firefighter's uniform. She says, "This is Captain James Morris Franklin of the Nevada fire marshal's office."

James Morris Franklin has millions of crisscross scars all over his face and dark circles under his eyes. His chin is covered with black and gray stubble, but not so much that you can't see his sagging jowls.

Suzanne says, "Captain Franklin, can you please explain to us what we are looking at. How did this fire get so out of control? And I hate to even ask this, but are those men safe?"

The wind picks up, and it takes a few seconds to get his equipment working. "Our men are well-trained. They know what to do. There are planes coming to drop some water."

Her face looks neutral—like this is just a story—but this is happening now with life on the line. She asks, "But what if the planes don't come?" I can tell she's scared. Even through the TV, I can see it in her eyes.

Dad throws the clicker across the room. "Where is the backup? The helicopters? He didn't have to be doing this. He could have stayed in school, where he would have been safe."

James Morris Franklin tugs at his scarred skin and looks up into the sky. He says, "I am sure they are on their way."

Suzanne cuts to Paul, the announcer in the studio, who says, "As soon as we know more, we will come back to California. Thanks, Suzanne, for that dramatic report. Until then, we will keep those brave firefighters in our thoughts."

A fire is a dangerous thing. It can explode without warning. I once read if you're close enough, it sounds like screaming.

The only thing we can do is wait.

Good things happen to bad people. Bad things happen to everyone.

But I always believed Mom was wrong, that she worried for nothing. No matter what Sam did, no matter what risks he took, he'd be fine.

Sam never failed. He was always in control. He fought for what was important to him. He was a hero. He was Superman.

At least, that's what I believed.

At 7:45, I wake up on the overstuffed recliner.

Mom points to the couch, where Dad is curled up, eyes closed, glasses still on. "Come to the kitchen. Let's let him sleep. He was up all night."

We tiptoe out of the room. Eat toast with butter and raspberry jelly. Mom even gives me a little bit of coffee for my milk. There is no news.

Mom's lips are bright jelly red. "I think that's a good thing. If he was dead, they would have had to notify us." There are raspberry seeds stuck between her teeth.

One more time, we call Sam's cell. We listen to his voice on the message, "This is Sam. You know what to do," and we start laughing/crying, because we really don't know what to do. Or say. Or think.

"Call us," Mom says. She squeezes my hand. "We love you."

We call the base too, but instead of a person, we get that odd ring that means the phone is disconnected. Or out of service. When we call the state office, the last resort, we find out that the town of Redding has turned off the power due to the enormity of the fires. Mom says, "Thanks for letting us know. Keep up the good work."

Strange. She's calm.

We do Dad's work. We go to the market, collect the donations, and mail a huge care package to all the fire-fighters at the base. She makes chocolate chip brownies from the mix. At noon, Dad finally wakes up. She cooks him a scrambled egg with cheese, toast, and a baked apple, which in the history of Fish breakfasts, might be a first.

Dad scrapes his plate. He jokes, "You know, I could use you on Sundays." But when the doorbell rings, he goes upstairs. "I'm just not ready for the well-wishers."

Neither am I, but Mom makes me stay. I talk to Mom's friends from the hospital and the entire staff at the restaurant. I call Mac, Soup, Eddie, and Coach, and they come over as fast as they can. Coach cancels practice. He says, "We took a vote and it was unanimous. We are not going to play until we know Sam is safe." When the rabbi walks in with three containers of soup, I get nervous. The rabbi never comes to your house when there is good news.

When he hugs me, he pats my back, and says something in Hebrew. I wait for him to bring up my Torah portion—to tell me how important it is to deal with tough tasks, but luckily he doesn't turn this into a lecture. He asks Mom, "What can I do? Would you like me to lead a healing prayer? Or do you want me to make phone calls."

"Don't make phone calls. Not yet." She tells the rabbi, "I hate that he thinks I'm not proud of him."

The rabbi opens his book. He talks for a long time about journeys that are worth something and the honor of responsibility. He says that nothing really good comes easy, and that God is with Sam right now, because God is righteous.

He says, "God never turns away from those in need."

But everyone knows that isn't really true. God lets good people die all the time. When good people are in need, sometimes God is looking the other way. I wish he would explain this.

Sometimes the good guy loses. Sometimes good men die.

That's why my dad writes to all those people.

The rabbi hands out copies of some prayers and invites everyone to join in. Some I know; some I don't. Mrs. Elliot sits next to Mom and sings along. Quietly. The rabbi sways back and forth.

After the last *Amen,* Mom gets up and goes to the kitchen, picks up one of the containers, opens it, and pours it into a saucepan. In the background, the TV stays on. The twenty-four-hour news stations discuss politics and theater, weather and one oil man's attempt to bring back the electric car. At three, they say the fire is twenty percent contained, and everyone cheers. By four, fifty percent. By seven, it is over.

Now we have to wait for a call. From Sam or a stranger. For the names. Every time the doorbell rings, I look away. I do not want to see a man in a uniform. I do not want someone to ask for Mr. and Mrs. Fish, the parents of Samuel Martin Fish of the Redding Five. I do not want to write a speech about the responsibility of remembering a brother who sacrificed his life, of a God who didn't hang around.

Mac, Eddie, and Soup sit in my room and play gin rummy and crazy eights—anything not to talk. Mac deals me the same three Jacks three times in a row.

Mac is usually a pretty good shuffler.

The next hand, he holds all the eights, and he doesn't even realize it.

He stares at the Wayne Timcoe poster. "Do you ever wonder what might have happened if Wayne Timcoe hadn't gotten injured?"

I don't answer—not because I don't have my theories, but because Coach is here. He sits on my bed. "You know, when Sam played for me, I just knew he was the kind of guy who was going to make a difference in somebody's life."

My mom comes in too, and we trade stories about Sam, all the oldies but goodies. Like the time he got caught driving the car . . . at age twelve. Or the time he threw a party when Mom and Dad were at services.

I say, "He offered me one hundred dollars if I could kick one goal past him. He gave me ten shots."

Coach laughs. "Did you do it?"

"Kick number eleven. It went right through his legs. He told me it was a sign that I was going to be just as good as he was."

Mom dabs her eye. "I told him I'd give him the money if he let his brother score."

Everyone laughs.

I excuse myself and go to Sam's room. Dad is there. He stands next to the words Sam painted on his wall.

Fight to the end.

Don't be a wuss.

Winning isn't everything . . . it's the only thing.

I say, "It was cool that you let him do that."

We look at Sam's trophies and jerseys, and his MVP certificate. Dad asks, "Do you think I expect too much from you? That I set the bar too high?"

"No. I don't know. What do you mean?"

My dad kisses the top of my head. "Your brother. There was never any stopping him. He was smart. And funny. And so athletic. It was such a disappointment when he dropped out of school. I guess I always thought this was a phase."

Now I am really scared. "What are you saying? Sam can do anything! Don't talk about him like he's not coming home. I bet he wasn't even scared. I bet he is already at the base, getting ready to call. I bet when Mom starts yelling at him about being an adrenaline junkie, he's going to say it was no big deal."

Dad smiles, but it's one of those sad smiles, the kind that makes people cry. "I hope you are right."

He sits on the bed. He holds the picture of me and Sam, the one from my room. "I'm just not ready for this. I am not ready for the call. I am not ready for a flag or an honor or a story about my great kid. I don't want to check the mail next week and find a letter from some guy who read my kid's obituary."

It's hard to watch your father cry.

There is no bad way to hear good news.

It is never too late at night to hear your brother's voice.

Mom picks up the phone on the first ring and puts it on speaker. "Hey everyone. It's me. I just wanted to tell you that I'm okay. I don't know if you saw this on the news, but we had a little bit of excitement."

It is Sam.

. . .

Mom pops open an old bottle of champagne, and she gives everyone—even me—a glass.

"To Sam!"

"To the Redding Region Five Smokejumpers!"

"To water!"

Dad calls the restaurant, and they bring over a cake. Five layers. All chocolate. We each take a huge slice.

On TV, the same news lady finally has an update. Now she reports from the studio.

The camera relives the nightmare. The sky, the fire, the houses. Then it shifts and we see piles of burnt rubble. Piles of charred wood. People sift through rubble to find anything they can salvage. Photographs. Toys.

There's nothing there.

Suzanne says, "What you see here is what is left of this once thriving, beautiful neighborhood. But today, no one is complaining. And that is because although seventy-five houses burned, everyone lived. All these families are safe. And I'm happy to tell you that the fourteen incredibly brave firefighters all survived. These men—these heroes—hung on until the planes arrived. Then—you're not going to believe this—they didn't go anywhere. They picked up their gear and fought the blaze until it was completely extinguished."

The anchor actually claps his hands. "Did they suffer injuries?"

"You are not going to believe this either, but they had

to be forced to go to the hospital for checkups. But it sounds like, besides some smoke inhalation, everyone is going to be fine, back on the job. They are America's bravest, and I am so glad they are all okay."

Dad turns the channel, and we listen to another station review the same story. They interview the base manager, who says, "My guys knew what to do. We train for exactly this type of situation. They are a team, and I'm proud of all of them."

After a while, the last slice of cake disappears. My parents' friends go home. Mac follows me to Sam's room. I sit on his bed and stare at Sam's trophies and slogans. I am so relieved. There are so many things Sam and I need to talk about. Luck. The team. Responsibility. I wonder what he was thinking about when the flames surrounded him. If he wished he could come home. And go back to school.

I wonder if he still thinks being a smokejumper is worth fighting for.

Mac wrings his hands, then wipes them on his jeans. "What's the matter?" I ask.

"Before anything else happens, I need to tell you something important." Mac says nothing for a long time. "Parker was right. I stole your card. I framed her. I did everything she said I did."

Jerry Mac MacDonald, the best player on our team, my friend, the luckiest guy I know, is a thief and a liar.

He apologizes profusely, over and over again. "All I can say is I'm sorry. I am really sorry. I was wrong. I was stupid. Will you ever be able to forget what I've done? Can you forgive me?"

On the one hand, an apology is a huge thing.

Just look at the presidents. Or even professional athletes.

Does anyone ever confess voluntarily?

No. They do not.

Until their guilt is firmly established, they lie. Until the proof is public.

Until they do not have a choice.

On the other hand, he stole my Wayne Timcoe card. He lied about Parker. He treated me like dirt. Retaliation would feel extremely satisfying.

I could hit him in the jaw. I could make him confess to his mom.

I could call Coach, who would definitely throw him off the team.

Then again, Dad is right. I am not always perfect. I need to shake hands with Mac. Say, "I accept your apology." Even if, in reality, I am still very mad, he is finally being honest. There is no reason to drag this out any more.

That's what the old Ari would do.

But that is the point. The old Ari did not do the right

thing. The old Ari did not accept his responsibility when it was given to him.

I don't want to be that person anymore.

I ask him, "Why?"

It is a simple question, but those are always the hardest to ask and answer.

For a moment, he says nothing. Then, "Honestly? When you found that card, your luck may have improved, but it messed me up. Suddenly, I couldn't do anything right. I couldn't play for beans. I felt tight. And nervous. And then the whole thing with Parker. When she started playing well and hanging out with you . . . I was jealous. I'm sorry, but I just wanted everything to be the way it used to be."

Maybe that's true. Maybe Mac did take his game for granted. Maybe he couldn't handle having an off day. But he used to have my back. And I had his. Always.

Honestly, I thought we did.

I am not convinced. "Do you really hate Parker that much? Why couldn't you let me be the star?"

We stand and stare at each other.

For a very long time.

Mac breaks the silence. "You will never understand."

When I ask him what that is supposed to mean, he paces around my room. "Can you just accept that I needed that lucky card. I had to have it . . . for a lot of reasons." He turns away.

That is a surprise. "A lot of reasons? Like what?"

"You know. Like my mom, who never comes to a game. Or Big Dave, who doesn't want to have anything to do with me. He couldn't care less what I do. Don't pretend you don't see. My family isn't like yours. Soccer is the only thing I am good at. It's the only thing."

This whole conversation makes my stomach ache. "You told me Big Dave took you fishing every week."

Mac says, "Yeah, I lied about that too. Like you didn't know."

"I didn't know."

He shakes his head hard, back and forth. I've never seen him this upset. "The funny thing is, when I had the card, everything was worse. Nothing went the way it was supposed to. And then even after you got it back, nothing was right. You didn't believe me. I could tell. You looked so miserable. Because of her. And then Sam got stuck in that fire." He rubs his eyes. "I never thought I'd say it, but I was sure I cursed him."

I don't confess that I was worried about the same thing. "You didn't have anything to do with that fire. It was just bad luck."

Coincidence.

Fate.

Like breaking your leg in a postgame celebration. Or finding the trading card you have wanted all your life.

"Thanks," he says. He thinks this is it. He apologized. He confessed. He finally told the truth.

Now it's my turn.

I tell Mac, "If you really want my forgiveness, you have to help me make this up to Parker." I have a simple plan.

When I tell him what we need to do, he doesn't look enthused.

I have to sell it. "She needs to feel that she is really part of our team. I can do that off the field. On the field, we have to give her a shot."

He is not buying. "Can't I do something else?"

It's a big moment. Normally, I would say yes.

But I think this is what the rabbi was talking about. I think this is where I need to do something new. "No," I say. "It's the only way. It's the only thing that will make things right with her. And me." When he still won't jump on board, I do not cave, even though I know it will change everything. "If you won't do it, do me a favor and don't show up for the game." I stand my ground. "Move up to premiere."

The next day at school, I tell everyone on the team. It is easy to keep this secret from Parker, because she will not stand within fifty feet of me. "Do you think we can pull it off? Will Mac really agree to do this?" Eddie asks.

The truth is, I have no idea. But I don't want to admit it. "He knows we all have to do things differently. We have to take our team in a new direction."

For the first time in a long time, Soup smiles. He says in an even, steady, totally low voice, "You sound almost presidential."

Saturday morning, that's what I think about. Not the presidents—but changing directions. Today is the day I will step out of Mac's shadow and be a leader.

When it is time to go to the field, I call him, but the machine picks up. It's not a good sign, but I refuse to think the worst. "See you at the game," I say after the beep.

When I hang up, I see my dad smiling at me. "Are you ready?" he asks. The paper has yet to arrive.

"I am ready." That is me, Ari Fish, presidential scholar and professional worrier taking the lead. It feels 180 degrees different. Scary. But good. Beyond good. A perfect personal U-turn.

TWENTY-SEVEN

"Nearly all men can stand adversity, but if you want to test a man's character, give him power."
—Abraham Lincoln

SOMERSET VALLEY vs. SETON SOUTH

SOMERSET VALLEY COMMUNITY FIELD

10 A.M.

Ronald Reagan better have been right when he said, "There is no limit to what you can accomplish if you don't care who gets the credit."

When Parker gets to the field, the plan begins.

First, I publicly apologize to her. I say, "Parker Llewellyn, I am sorry. I was wrong to blame you. I knew you would never take my card. You are a great player." She rolls her eyes and looks the other way. It is hard to keep a straight face, but I do it. Everything is working just the way I planned. I do not smile when I ask her if she wants to count presidents with us.

She says, "I think I'd rather just sit here and stretch."

I say, "I was an idiot."

She says, "You are immature."

When I promise I'll grow up, she puts her hands on her hips and tosses her hair back and forth. "Do me a favor, and let's just play the game."

Girls. They take a long time to get over stuff.

I was counting on that.

Coach keeps his pregame pep talk short and right on point. Mac still is not here. "Okay, team, let's stick it to them. Destroy them. Pound them. Send them home crying. I want this one more than a spring day in the middle of February." The truth is none of this is necessary. We are all feeling extremely motivated. Seton South displays their big silver championship plate on the opposite side of our field. No one has to remind us what happened in Mooretown.

He assigns positions. Defense first. Then offense. But he does not call Mac's name. "Where is he?" Eddie asks. "Ari, I thought you said—"

"Didn't he tell you?" Coach asks. "Mac has finally decided to take the plunge and move up to the premiere league. If you have a chance, you should all go out this afternoon and cheer him on."

It is a hit. A slap in the face. Not just to me—but to all of us.

While Coach talks to the offense, everyone, even

Parker, looks down at the grass. They look dejected, like there is no point in playing.

But they are wrong.

I step forward into the middle of the huddle and look at my teammates' nervous, worried faces. "Are you afraid we can't win without him?" I look at each player on my team. "Because we can." This is my Emancipation Proclamation, my Gettysburg Address, my Great Society, my Inaugural Address. "So Mac isn't here. So what! We are more than one great player. We are a team." I point to the field and point out every player's strengths. "Now let's show everybody what we can do."

When Coach pumps his fist, I say, "Let's give them something special to watch."

The whistle blows, and Soup takes control of the ball. Right away, he motions to Parker and they run toward the goal. They pass the ball back and forth, across and forward. Soup looks taller. David keeps up. Parker fools her defender with a very beastly crossover. When she takes her first shot, the crowd goes crazy. Her second shot hits the bar and ricochets right to the stopper. Coach yells, "That's the way to break their D! Next time, you'll get them!"

All that practicing has paid off.

My plan is going to work.

We definitely don't need Mac.

Eddie can't believe how much room Parker has. "You

were right," he says. She takes the ball down the lane uncontested. "She is good."

And fast.

She definitely knows how to handle a defense.

Off the field, Parker Llewellyn may never like any of us. She may never trust us, or want to drink milkshakes with us, or give us another chance. She may never forgive me, no matter what I say or do. But even she will have to admit that on the field, right now, we are united. Seton South looks completely discombobulated.

You can call it luck, and that's definitely part of it. But it's not the whole truth. Not by a long shot.

The truth about soccer is that one great player is nice to have, but a team that works together will never go down easy.

I finally understand.

The next time he has the ball, Soup doesn't hesitate. He passes the ball directly to Parker.

And this time, she doesn't miss.

After the final whistle, three reporters run over to talk to the first girl in boys' select soccer history to score five goals against a championship team. She grabs me by the arm. "Wait for me? Okay?"

I sit under the elm tree. I hear her tell the reporters, "I am so glad that I was able to show all of New England that girls can play in any league."

Her father brags. "Just you watch and wait. This little

girl is going to be a star. She's got the talent and the drive."

By the time they are done, it is noon, and the air is cold. The grass is starting to look brown. One reporter notices me. "How does it feel to play on a team with someone like Parker Llewellyn?"

I say, "Great. Parker is an excellent player, and—"

"Thanks. That's nice." He doesn't even bother asking my name, which Parker finds atrocious. And extremely funny.

Her father asks, "Are you the mastermind of this media onslaught?"

I act innocent. "Can you believe our very own sports reporters had no idea that a girl was playing in the boys' league?" I try not to blush. "After that, it was all Parker."

"I couldn't have done it without help." She looks into the empty parking lot. "That last assist was unnecessary. Soup had a wide-open shot."

Her father and I say at the same time, "Yours was better." When she smiles, Parker Llewellyn is exceptionally pretty.

"Still—"

"Still nothing," he says, lifting her off her feet into a hug. "Parker, today is your day. I'm going home. Maybe we should go get a steak at Central Station? I heard they make a great filet." He winks. "So don't keep your old man waiting. Keep today's practice short."

I say, "Practice?" I don't believe it. "Parker, seriously— and I mean seriously—you don't have to practice. From now on, this is how we play. The slate is clean. We are one team. We practice and play together."

I expected her to be happy. Or maybe mad. I thought she might hold all of this against me.

She doesn't. Parker Llewellyn starts to cry. It's just a little at first, but I really don't know what to do. By the time her father has pulled out of the parking lot, her eyes are bright red, and when she looks at me, way up close, I wonder if she might even kiss me.

She doesn't do that either.

Instead, she sits down, looks away, and pulls at the dead grass. "Ari, I have something important to tell you." When I don't say anything, she says, "I don't know how to tell you this, but I haven't been completely honest."

This was not what I was expecting.

She says, "Please promise me you're not going to be mad." An old gray sedan parks in the farthest spot.

She stands. And waves to the driver of the car. "I swear, I wanted to tell you." She extends her hand and helps me up. "I was dying to. But then, well, I couldn't. And when the season started, my dad told me that I shouldn't give up this advantage . . . that no one was doing me any favors. And then you started acting like a jerk, and then, well . . . it got complicated."

I am so confused.

She waves again to the guy in the car. "I want you to meet someone."

After two more waves, a man gets out and walks

toward us. He has a slight limp. Mirrored aviator sunglasses. A black T-shirt.

My brain is on overdrive. "Is that Beer Man?"

"Yes." She laughs, a little. "Just promise me right now you won't be mad."

"I won't be mad."

When he steps on the field, she says to him, "You have to explain to him that I had to keep your secret. Tell him I had no choice. That there was no other way."

Now he looks mad. "You do know what this means."

And now she looks like she is going to cry again. "I know. But I have to tell him. This is what I want."

"Okay then. I'll confirm," Beer Man says. "We had a deal." He crosses his arms over his chest. "We still do." She leans into him and hugs him, and for a second, he can't help smiling. "By the way, great game today, kid."

I ask, "You were here?"

"Always. Every game. Wouldn't miss it."

His voice sounds different. Not Southern, the way it did when he talked to me at the game.

I don't tell Parker that. "Am I missing something? How do you know each other?"

Parker smiles and grabs my arm. She tells Beer Man, "Take off your glasses. And those dumb gloves."

There is a small scar near his eye.

And a ring on his finger. It is a big ring, encrusted with diamonds. An All-Star Soccer ring, the kind reserved for champions.

"It can't be."

Parker looks extremely nervous. "Ari, I'd like to introduce you to the person who has helped me perfect my game, to the best player I have ever met. Ari Fish, meet Wayne Timcoe."

I am in shock. Beer Man is Wayne Timcoe.

My hero is the beer delivery man.

"Ari, say something," Parker says. "Shake hands. Say hello. Don't just stand there."

Wayne's hand is huge, just like Sam said.

This has to be a joke. "You are Wayne Timcoe? You drive my mom crazy. How can you be Wayne Timcoe? You've been here all this time."

He kicks some dirt. Looks off into the distance. Mumbles, "Your mom should learn to drive."

How many times had I watched the black truck roll by and wished he was someone extraordinary? But this is a total letdown. Beer Man could have been anyone else in the world and that would have been okay.

I hope my face does not give me away, but this does not seem right.

I don't know what to say to him. Parker looks extremely nervous, which isn't exactly helping. I ask her, "How did you figure it out?"

She looks at Wayne, and they both nod and she laughs. "I didn't have to figure anything out," she says. "Wayne is my dad's cousin. I have known him all my life." She grabs him by the elbow, and he—Wayne Timcoe—I still don't believe it—gives her a huge hug. He smiles the way he did when he was interviewed on ESPN after his first pro win. "It's one of the reasons we moved here. So he could give me lessons."

Wayne says, "But only if they kept my secret."

Parker starts to apologize again, but I get it. "So he's the friend you've been practicing with?"

"Yep."

"The one you didn't want me to play with?"

She bites her lip. "Do you understand why?"

Now I smile. "I would have done exactly the same thing."

Parker says, "You know. My dad. He won't be satisfied until I am the best."

"Your old man was always the most competitive of all of us," Wayne says. "Never would let any of us forget that he could have played in the league too, if he hadn't decided to go to college."

I dig through my backpack. Before anything else happens, I have to show him the card, wrapped in Sam's message. "Will you sign it?" I ask. I cross my fingers. I wish I had a camera. Or a cell phone. I wish I could call Sam right now, tell him that Beer Man was Wayne Timcoe and that he was standing next to me.

He wouldn't believe it.

Wayne stares at the card, like he's never seen one before. "You'd think the league would give one to you, but they don't."

Parker hands him a pen. When I start to spell my name, he shakes his head. "Don't take this personally, but I don't do dedications."

He writes: *Wayne Timcoe.*

It is almost illegible. I am about to take it very personally, when he draws a soccer ball coming toward a net, right over the blue and red stripe.

It is the most unbelievable, fantastic, lucky thing that has ever happened to me. I say, "But I don't understand why you are hiding. If people knew you were here all this time, they'd go crazy. You wouldn't have to deliver beer."

"What's wrong with delivering beer?" He crosses his hands over his chest. "It's an honest living."

"But you are Wayne Timcoe. You are a legend. A hero. If you didn't want anyone to recognize you, why did you come back?"

Wayne looks at Parker, and she nods. "Tell him," she says. "He'll understand."

He sighs. "When I knew that my career was finished, I went through some pretty bad times. I did some things that I'm not really proud of. Got in a heap of trouble." He looks off into space, and I look at his eye. His chin. His hands. He rubs them together. "I needed a job fast, so I called Will. I always loved that black truck." At first, I am sure he's joking, but Wayne Timcoe does not look like the kind of guy who clowns around.

"But all you had to do was call Coach. Or the school. You are famous. You're our hero."

He turns to face the field. "That's not my doing."

Across the field and up, voices interrupt us. Parker grabs Wayne by the elbow and points to a large crane rising up to meet the double *x*. "Look at that. They are finally fixing the *x*'s."

That is not the only job being done. A small group of men drag ladders to the old blue and yellow scoreboard, the one that reads "Home of Wayne Timcoe." They carry cans of paint. White paint. They start to paint over the banner.

I say, "They can't do that."

Wayne says, "Yes they can. I think it's time."

We watch the word *home* disappear. Then *Tim*. When all that is left is *coe,* I almost begin to cry.

I say, "Wayne—can I call you that? Maybe some people have forgotten you, but I haven't. I think about you all the time. You made it! To the pros! If you just let people know who you are, it would make such a big difference to our team. And our town."

Parker says she has told him the same thing many times. "Please, Wayne, if you won't listen to me, listen to him. It's the truth."

Now the entire sign is white. The letters look like shadows. One more coat and his name will be gone.

I hold the card in my hand. I stare at his writing. I look at Wayne the man, the beer man, the local hero, the soccer star. Parker says, "Please stay. It would mean a lot to us."

I add, "To the whole town."

He looks at Parker. "Sorry, kid. You knew the deal."

He turns away and limps to his car. Parker and I do nothing. We stare at the field and the crane and the plain white sign.

When he slams his car door, the x's light up red, white, and blue.

It's got to be a sign.

The next day, Wayne Timcoe is gone. There is a new Beer Man and he does not wear shades. Actually, Beer Man is a Beer Woman, and she has blond hair and wears really tight jeans. Eddie thinks she's hot. She beeps at all the kids while she waits at the crosswalk. And she set up a donation box next to mine.

HALLOWEEN TREATS! PLEASE DONATE!

It's for kids who are in the hospital. The second he saw it, Dad donated five batches of his famous only-in-October orange chocolate brownies to the cause.

Parker is the only person who is still positive that Wayne will come back. She says, "He just needs some time to think it out." After every practice, we sit under the elm tree, hoping he will show up. "My dad says he has done this kind of thing before. He says if he was planning on never coming back, he would have left me a note."

We win the next two games.

We lose a game. The Home of Wayne Timcoe sign now reads: "Somerset Valley supports our troops." On either side they have painted a ribbon.

We stay late to look for him. After school and practice. He never comes home. For that matter, neither does Sam.

He is the only person I tell. Sam says, "That is the most completely random thing I have ever heard."

"Random?"

He coughs really loud. "Yeah. Random. Unpredictable. Haphazard. Arbitrary. I think a lot of things are like that. You have to admit, you have to be really brave to walk away from instant fame. I admire that."

These are interesting concepts, but right now, there are more important questions to ask.

"When are you coming home? Will you please come watch me play?" I wouldn't normally ask, but the Northern California fires are officially contained. Page two yesterday morning. I figure they can spare my brother for a few days.

I cross my fingers. I say "Please" until he stops laughing. I send him an e-mail that says: "Sam, I really want you to see me play."

At first, he doesn't say no or yes. When I tell him that Mom will buy his ticket home, he sighs, like this was all for her.

"I'm sorry. I wish I could, buddy." He has a lot of excuses. He reminds me that there is still a lot of work to be done, that just because the newspapers say the fires

240

are contained does not mean they're out. And of course, there are new fires to extinguish in the southern part of the state, and they're just as bad and undermanned as the northern ones. Sam says, "The guys need me. And I can't let them down."

"Please. Just one game. One day. You haven't been home in so long. Don't they have to give you leave once in a while?" I lay on the guilt. "We may make it to the finals. It would mean a lot to me."

But Abraham Lincoln did not know everything. Not all men can be swayed by honey. At least, not Sam. "No. I'm sorry. It would be great to see you play, but I just can't." He says nothing for so long that I wonder if he is still on the other end of the phone. "Look, Ari. You're old enough to understand. I'll see you at the bar mitzvah. But other than that, I am not coming home."

"What do you mean? Is it because of Mom? Because she wants you to go back to college?" That doesn't seem very brave.

"It's just easier." He sighs. "I can't deal with her expectations. It's too much."

"Are you kidding me?" I say. Lately, I seem to be confused all the time. "You should hear her brag about you. She thinks you're the bravest oldest son she has."

He doesn't laugh. "She thinks I'm wasting my life. Ruining my best years." He sounds tired. And mad. "You know, around here no one thinks I need a graduate degree. Or anything else."

Now I am beyond confused. "I thought you said you quit school because you wanted to do something important with your life."

Sam says, "I do. And I am. But I also had to get away." He sighs a third time. "Out here, I fit in. Out here, in the middle of a fire, being the best doesn't matter. Here, I just need to do my job."

I think about Wayne. And Mac. "I think I understand. But are you sure you can't come? Just one game? I'll tell Mom not to bug you."

Now he laughs. "No, buddy. I wish I could, but I can't."

I tell him it's okay—that I totally respect how he feels—but what he doesn't know: This stinks. I'm mad. I don't care if he's the greatest firefighter on the planet or not. I don't care if he could be a doctor or whatever else Mom wants him to be.

Right now, more than anything, I just wish he'd do the right thing, come home and be my brother.

In class the next day, I pass notes to Parker, David, Soup, and Eddie. They all say the same thing. "Please come to my house for a very important announcement."

Parker shows up first. We hang around in the backyard. She kicks. I save. Sometimes, I even let her score.

No bribery necessary.

David, Eddie, and Soup show up after dark. It no longer feels weird not to include Mac, but we still aren't totally comfortable talking about what happened. Ever since Mac went premiere, he's been eating lunch with new friends at a new table. He gets a ride to school. He doesn't talk to us.

The last thing I said to him was, "I wish you could have helped us out. But that was your choice, and this is mine."

The last thing he said to me was, "If you don't win, don't come crying to me."

It was pretty anticlimactic.

Eddie and Soup sit on the grass and laugh. Soup is telling him a joke none of us have ever heard before. Parker heads the ball past my knees. David shows up late. "You said it was urgent?"

I leave the ball in the net. "I wanted you guys to be here to witness something really important."

It's going to hurt. Worse than anything I've ever done before. I have thought about every possible alternative, and this is it. I am determined to do it. I have to do it.

I will never take the next step until I stand completely on my own.

So I take the card out of its protective pocket.

I kiss it one last time and say, "Good-bye, Wayne Timcoe."

Then before anyone can talk me out of it, I fold it in two. Then I rip it into tiny pieces.

And then, very carefully, in an ashtray, far away from any tree . . .

I burn it.

TWENTY-EIGHT

"Change will not come if we wait for some other person or some other time. We are the ones we've been waiting for. We are the change that we seek."
—Barack Obama

Hey Steve!

I am a Revolution fan who also loves the Pats, the Celtics, and the Sox.

You often write about the importance of role models and heroes, and up until now, I've had a few. They were people I looked up to. I wanted to be just like them. But one by one, they all let me down.

It's pretty depressing.

The thing that makes me mad—they all could have done important things. But instead, each of them did the easy thing. They ran away. They decided that they had better things to do than be a hero.

I still admire their accomplishments,

but the truth is, it's not the same. It makes me sad. And mad. I used to look up to these people. I thought they were brave. Maybe I expected them to be perfect. My mom thinks I'm the one who changed.

So I guess my question is: What do you do when you realize your hero is just a regular guy with regular problems? What do you do when you realize that your hero can be sort of a jerk? Once your role model has disappointed you—even if he makes you really mad—do you have to stop looking up to him totally?

Regards,
An avid reader

The morning of the last game of the season, our entire team shows up at my house. We eat blueberry muffins and instead of counting presidents, we talk about Barack Obama, who likes to talk about change, even though he has said many times that he also likes history.

Eddie says, "And so, my fellow Americans, ask not what your team can do for you, but what you can do for your team."

Very funny.

I put on my U Mass T-shirt, but it's not about superstition. It's the only one that's clean. In less than six months, I will become a bar mitzvah. Mom thinks I'm old enough to do my own laundry.

We walk to the field together.

If we don't win, we go home with a seven and two record. We will sign up for spring soccer with our heads held high.

If we win, we play the weekend before Thanksgiving for the big silver plate.

Halfway there, I realize I didn't even read my horoscope.

The day is perfect—yellow sun and no clouds. The leaves have fallen off the elm tree, so there is very little shade. The double x shines day and night, and it must get hot up there, because the crows don't perch there anymore. They stick to the tree and the telephone wires.

It's been three weeks since Wayne Timcoe left, two weeks since Parker announced that we could stop hoping he would show up, and one week since I stopped waiting for Sam to call to tell us to pick him up at the airport.

In the huddle, we talk about winning and working together.

Coach says, "Listen people, today's a big day and there's a lot at stake. But I don't want you to measure your success by the results of today alone. I want you all to know that, just in case we don't cross the finish line victorious, I have enjoyed almost every minute of this season together."

In moments like this, Coach can get pretty flowery.

He says, "Listen, team. I want that plate. You know I want it bad. It's been ten years since I held it in my hands, and I'm aching to hold it over my head." He hands out a bunch of compliments and platitudes, but I am too pumped up to listen. Until the end. He says, "But team, remember, even if it isn't in the cards, I want you to know you are a great team. One of the strongest I've ever had the privilege to coach."

We clap our hands. We take our places. I tell him to stop worrying. We are a great team. And we all want to win. We will win.

He should know: That has nothing to do with cards.

SOMERSET VALLEY VS. PLAINFIELD/MONTROSE

—— SEMIFINALS ——

SOMERSET VALLEY COMMUNITY FIELD
10 A.M.

POW!

Smack!

The ball hits my hands hard. I pick it up and kick it straight to Eddie, who kicks it to Parker to Old to Soup.

No team gets to the finals without a little bit of skill.

Plainfield/Montrose has some nice shooters, and they keep me busy, but they are no match for our two man–one woman front.

At the half, we are up by three, and Coach is reclining in the lawn chair. Mischelotti is down to a walking cast, and he runs up and down the field, shouting directions. Soup, Old, and Parker have scored. When Coach calls us to the net, he has tears in his eyes.

Real tears.

He's never done that before.

He says, "You kids are great. You've got fire. You've got speed. Fish, you and Biggs are making it look easy. And the offense looks stupendous. Uncatchable. Unstoppable. Unbelievable."

It's no fluke.

He points to two yellow and blue coolers. "I've got ice cream and sodas for when we win. Chef Fish over there has made an unbelievable victory feast that we don't want to waste." My parents wave, two thumbs up, and Dad wipes his eyes and nods toward the elm tree. "We also have a special guest assistant coach to pump you up."

I know before I see him.

From behind the tree, he steps out. He wears mirrored aviator sunglasses. He's got a small limp that is almost undetectable. His vintage Somerset Valley Soccer jersey is tight around the shoulders. A red and blue scarf is tied around his head.

He's got a ball in his right hand.

He crouches low in the old familiar pose.

Parker puts her hands over her mouth. "He's here."

I run as fast as I can.

"Hey buddy."

I pull off the rag and feel his porcupine hair. His shoulders are huge. Almost too big for the rest of him. When you have shoulders like that, you can lug seventy pounds of gear in extreme heat. You can help your brothers survive when a fire explodes.

You can come home.

"Nice timing, Sam."

We are exactly the same height.

He rubs my head too. "When I thought about it, there was no way I could miss watching the new champions at work."

We jog toward the rest of the team. I do the introductions. "This is my brother, Sam. He is a smokejumper for the Redding Region Five Smokejumpers. Their mission is to care for the land and serve the people. They are the ultimate team players."

Sam takes a low bow. He says, "I am proud to be here." He's humble. So am I. Humble and happy. Especially when Parker says, "You guys look exactly alike."

That makes me beyond happy.

Coach pulls the huddle together. "I thought I'd let Sam here talk to you today."

Sam shakes Coach's hand. Then they slap each other five and laugh, like they have a private joke. He looks over us and puffs up his chest. Turkey. "I used to play for this guy and this team, and my brother keeps telling me you are among the best in the league."

Coach says, "One of the best I've ever seen."

Sam nods. "So then, I don't have to tell you, soccer is a game of timing and skill. But it is also a game of—"

"Sam," I interrupt. "I don't want to be disrespectful, but we have worked hard. We play together. We are about to slaughter Plainfield/Montrose. I think we know the truth about soccer. At least, we know how to play like a team." I put my hand into the middle, and so does everyone else.

Parker's is right on top of mine.

We yell, "Somerset Valley rules." And take the field.

Sam walks with me to the net. "So what do you think the presidents would say to you now?"

Probably a lot. But I don't need them. Not today.

My parents are on the sidelines and my brother is here. I have friends. We have a team.

That is all the luck I need.

ACKNOWLEDGMENTS

Although I was never particularly athletic, I have always liked watching and talking and writing about sports. I find everything about the game compelling: the shifts in momentum, the effort, the highlights, and of course, the characters. I appreciate the concept of team—that no one player can win the game alone. Certainly, that was true for this book. As I wrote and rewrote and re-imagined these characters and situations, there were many shifts in momentum and game plan. I required the humor and support and advice of many trusted friends.

My sincere gratitude goes out to my editor, Liz Waniewski, as well as Heather Alexander and the entire team at Dial Books. Thank you for loving and believing in Ari Fish from the very start. Your unwavering support and enthusiasm made this story stronger. Your confidence made me a better writer.

To my agent, Sarah Davies. Timing is everything. You asked me about "feet of clay" and look what happened—a great assist! Thank you.

Hugs and cheers to my friends who write, who took time out of their busy lives to read and critique this story: Kim Marcus, Zu Vincent, Kellye Carter Crocker, Elly Swartz, Ammi Joan Paquette, Cindy Faughnan, Bethany Hegedus, Margaret Bechard, Uma Krishnaswami, and Louise Hawes. For good conversations and fearless support: Nancy Werlin, Franny Billingsley, Toni Buzzeo, Kathi Appelt, Carolyn Coman, Tim Wynne-Jones, Cynthia Leitich Smith, Mary Atkinson, and the luckiest writers in the universe—the students and alumni of Vermont College. There is no better cheering squad than my writers.com writers—you inspire and stretch me—as well as the attendees of the eight (and counting) novel writing retreats at Vermont College. This book might still be a manuscript in a drawer if it were not for the encouragement, enthusiasm, and insight of Tami Lewis Brown.

For getting me away from my desk, sharing rides, and talking about anything but writing, thank you to my friends in Hanover, NH—Gail, Deb, Devora, Karla, Lisa, Marjorie, Jill, Sharon, and Sarah—and the entire staff at the Hanover Co-op. Thanks to John Kemp Lee, keeper of the Bill Buckner (everyone has a bad day once in a while) baseball card, and to Pam Takiff and Ethan Wilcox, who bravely read very early versions. I discovered a lot about Ari working with my fabulous dvar girls: Lizzie, Sydney, Sara, Bonnie, and Hannah. And Parker would not be Parker if it were not for one crazy carpool with Amanda Washington.

A big whopping hug to Tanya Lee Stone, for being present for every step of this crazy journey. I am so proud of everything you have accomplished. No sports analogies necessary. I am so grateful to have a friend like you.

To my family: Rich and Judy Aronson, Miriam, Anne, Brian, Rachael, and Aaron, who supplied necessary insider information. Massive hugs and kisses to Rebecca, Liz, and Ed for unfailing support, solidarity, love and humor, and making your parents look extremely competent! I am so excited to see what each of you will do next.

Dear Elliot: thank you for sharing your passion for history, as well as your interest in the presidents and presidential trivia. I don't remember how or when you discovered Cormac O'Brien's *Secret Lives of the U.S. Presidents,* but meals haven't been the same since! Every day, you teach me something new. I really hope you like this book.

And last, to my husband, Michael. Thank you for embracing our family and giving us safety and music and happiness and stability. Your trust in me is the greatest gift. Every day I wake up knowing I am beyond lucky.